The Optimistic Existentialist

Richard V. Campagna

1st WORLD
PUBLISHING

THE OPTIMISTIC EXISTENTIALIST

RICHARD V. CAMPAGNA

© Richard V. Campagna 2006

Published by 1stWorld Publishing
1100 North 4th St. Suite 131, Fairfield, Iowa 52556
tel: 641-209-5000 • fax: 641-209-3001
web: www.1stworldpublishing.com

First Edition

LCCN:
SoftCover ISBN: 1-59540-880-0
HardCover ISBN: 1-59540-879-7
eBook ISBN: 1-59540-881-9

All rights reserved. No part of this book may be reproduced or utilized in any form or by any means, electronic or mechanical, including photocopying or recording, or by any information storage and retrieval system, without permission in writing from the author.

This material has been written and published solely for educational purposes. The author and the publisher shall have neither liability or responsibility to any person or entity with respect to any loss, damage or injury caused or alleged to be caused directly or indirectly by the information contained in this book.

The characters and events described in this text are intended to entertain and teach rather than present an exact factual history of real people or events.

Dedicated to "my" family specifically and "the" family in general. When it really counts, if anyone really cares, they are the only ones who give a damn if you swim or sink in the rectum of hell.

"There is no pleasure so great as that which you feel you will not be enjoying for much longer."

— Tacitus, Roman historian

And its corollary:

"There is no pain so bearable as that which you believe you will not be enduring for much longer."

"All ill winds blow some good fate."

—From Silas Marner by George Eliot

I Search For A Woman ...

I search for a woman who'l let me be me,
As I am in search of becoming,
Who'll let me react without wedging me in,
As this lawn-mower mind keeps on humming.

Every step that I take, every move that I make,
Can't be judged, only blindly accepted,
Every time I fuck off, or around or fuck up,
I'll have faith that I won't be rejected.

Only deep in my grave will I truly be known,
Only then will my love know her lover,
In my life she could never quite know what she loved,
So in doubt would she wallow and hover.

Loving me, you now see, would mean taking a chance,
Since there's never a guide for to follow,
And I think that the reason I've not found true love,
Is cause true love's not easy to swallow.

Foreword

I recall an episode which occurred a hefty thirty-eight years ago and I invite you to join me in my memories....

I was tired and understandably beat as I muscled my way out of the Palace Theatre in New York City. I was smack in the middle of Broadway.

The insensitivity of the show I'd just seen would render it an inevitable flop and the unsophisticated acting and directing suggested to me that the entire cast of "Get Your Rocks Off Momma" would be spending a long, unrewarding summer on a shuttle bus between Albany and Pawtucket, Rhode Island. All I had in mind at that moment was getting my throbbing body to a soft mattress as expeditiously as possible, but the closest bed appeared to be my own mahogany double in the Park Slope section of Brooklyn, such bed incidentally, not having seen a man since the Republicans were deemed to be honest. Man or no man, I longed for my checker-board pillow, and the realization that a fifty-minute trek stood between my mushrooming fatigue and potential bedroom bliss loomed heavy on my mind.

No sooner had I begun to chart my course of action than I was catapulted into a temporary state of nothingness, and upon regaining control of my faculties I realized that the throngs had whisked me across 43rd Street and had deposited me in front of the HOUSE OF MUFFINS.

"What in the name of Jehovah is a HOUSE OF MUFFINS?" said my misfiring ego to my superego, then on sabbatical.

"Who the hell cares? Go on in and have a cup of coffee!" retorted my id. I did.

A vast empty counter. Sticky coffee stains abounded. Surprisingly enough however, no vomit-inducing odors. A balding effeminate man was preparing prepackaged HOUSE OF MUFFIN coffee, with patches of grease floating atop each finished pot, and was simultaneously arranging various kinds of pastry and Danish, a woeful majority of which were adorned with mold. I opted for toast and tea.

Enter, one 5'10" well-dressed young man, burdened with legal treatises and a monstrous maroon text entitled "Readings in Jurisprudence." He sat himself down, directly to my right and began a piecemeal attack on a green pamphlet with the title "New York Business Corporation Law."

"Coffee and a danish," he muttered, oblivious to the fact that grease and mold were necessary adjuncts to his snack. Then he returned to his work.

Enter, one full-fledged prostitute who spoke a rare dialect of English-a soulful hybrid of South Brooklynese and a Savannah drawl. Short and somewhat dumpy this young woman had extremely pleasant features although her Raggedy-Ann fall tended to cheapen her appearance a trifle. She, like myself, ordered some tea with honey and lemon and an order of toast dripping with butter.

Personally, I was still somewhat dazed, the young law student was industriously digesting the rules for filing certificates of incorporation and the hooker was simultaneously trying to hook our sociological jurisprude, with recurring glances of desperation.

My cloudiness vanished abruptly. I was in the thick of an existential encounter between "MAN" (Calvin Labozzetta was plastered across the young law student's torts notebook) and "WHORE." No doubt she was one. But would he likewise show himself to be the same. The ensuing dialogue was straightforward and chock full of meaning. I was so glad I didn't duck into CHOCK FULL OF NUTS.

"Hey baby, you just get outah school?"

"No, I've been studying all day and decided to do a little hanging out."

"Yah, well wayah you all plannin' to do the rest o' you hangin' out?"

"At home, studying some commercial law. Any objections?"

"Yah, you ain't got no woman?"

"Not right now, my dear. I'm studying law right now, planning for my future. And if I weren't studying I wouldn't 'get' me a woman, I'd 'encounter' one."

"Shit mothah-fucka. Any dude talkin'like that gotta be kind of faggy. See that dude behind the counter. You queer like him?" Dead silence.

Calvin arose with a jerk and a smirk so enigmatic that neither shrink nor sage, nor prophet, nor Edgar Cayce himself could have predicted what would come next.

He lunged for her 54¢ check, ripped it into sixteen very

equal pieces and laid down the cash to cover it, tip included. He gathered the multifarious texts, canned briefs and restatements he'd scattered on the counter and stared blankly at his insultor. Suddenly, with incredible dexterity and precision did he grab her left breast, so as to preclude any motion on her part yet so as not to produce any substantial pain. She sat there mummified, her huge breast clothed in dacron and wedged in between his bony, hairy Italian fingers and almost having its nipple dunked, inside his lukewarm coffee. He spoke to her loudly and clearly, probably intending that this particular prostitute never forget the crossing of their paths. Even if she does in fact forget his ultimate words to her, Calvin may rest assured that I never will.

"You my dear are a strumpet by profession. And that's not so rare since by profession most of us are. I, as an attorney, may prove to be a bigger and a better one than you'll ever be, especially with flabby tits like these. (He briskly jiggled her left breast). But in our private lives we are not whores in any sense. We're developing human beings seeking what it is that we truly are. We call this the search for our essence. Anyone who denies to us this search or who makes us feel guilty for the dynamics of our particular search we call a Fascist-a Fascist pig. As a lawyer, I'll fight like a fiend for the rights of others to procure your services if that's what makes them happy and for your right to render such services. I'll always fight for the rights of all persons to trip onward through life, free from developmental shackles in optimistic fashion. In turn I expect you, my little jewel, to treat with decency others who just don't happen to require your services to find their essence. The tea's on me baby. And have a Happy New Year!"

And he vanished into the permeable masses on Broadway.

Richard V. Campagna

I finished my tea and just sat on my stool, stupefied, as the girl began to cry relentlessly. For those fleeting moments, however, at the tragic expense of the hooker's feelings, Calvin Labozzetta had given absolute meaning to my fragilely constructed reality.

If he'd only gone around the corner and offered his plot, theme and dramatic charisma to the cast of "Get Your Rocks Off Momma" he'd have saved them the long, hot summer of '69 where they were reputed to have played to thirty-five half-empty high school auditoriums from Booth Bay Harbor, Maine down to sun-baked Ocala, Florida.

My subsequent sleep on the D train back to Brooklyn, with my New York Post propped 'neath my cranium was better than my usual snooze on my checkerboard pillow. Calvin Labozzetta had saved the day ...

Life has swept me along since the Labozzetta episode, or in the alternative I have humbly dragged it on along with me, and I must ashamedly admit that for almost forty years no one has had such a profound influence on my psyche as Calvin, but for the quasi-imaginary character of Martin P. Feinstein, created by Richard Campagna, in the work you are about to read.

For those of you who weren't lucky enough to have been with me in December of 1968, or to have met a Calvin Labozzetta of your own, Martin P. Feinstein in action will do the trick. I'm overjoyed that Richard allowed me to be the first to read this work, and I know that after reading it you'll be better able to spar with human complexity and paradox and fashion an optimistic solution, as was I. Enough said.

Jackie Nadohl

Preface

Tonite I was thinking to myself, "What kind of people will be far out enough to read your book?" I couldn't really come up with anything concrete but I didn't really give a shit. I was fascinated just to contemplate a potential merger of souls, via the vehicle of a novel, without the inefficient nonsense of role-playing and inter-personal strategic warfare. With this work, through my created character, I can lay down my cards and there's no immediate fear of getting trumped. I assume I've stumbled across one of the therapeutic joys of fiction writing, and for the sake of my revived literary career I hope there are countless other rewarding moments.

If you've gotten this far into this book you've got to be asking yourself at least two questions. Who is this author and what has he got in mind with this alleged novel?

I'm a lawyer, a literature buff, a lover (aren't we all), a linguist, a libertarian and a trained manipulator, no longer practicing. I'm also an ex-pinball freak, an avid basketball fan and a world traveler. At times I'm extremely secure, although at times the pendulum swings to the other extreme. Sometimes I'm cute, sometimes I'm even handsome and oftentimes I'm actually downright unattractive.

All of the above, however, are labels which people use to describe me. They're afraid to chomp upon, no less digest the possibility that someone who they actually know and admire in certain ways can be lacking a clearly defined and colored-in role. The Venus Paradise coloring pencils haven't yet made me into the portrait depicted in their guide books, and probably never will.

People are actually afraid to accept me for what I really am—a human being with very diffuse and untested values in many arenas, though not in all. It's a frightening thought for most Americans. To them, a man who can occasionally be a glasslike void, a transparent wanderer with no direction is a nut; he's reduced to a loathsome and semi-dangerous psychotic, to be set aside into whatever vessel will hold him.

I am not a total glass man. I have some degree of opaqueness on the periphery. I am a lawyer and I believe in the ethics of the profession when practiced properly, although such is becoming increasingly difficult to accomplish due to an all pervasive "judicial, political and journalistic realism" overtaking our legal system as well as our culture. I am a linguist and believe in the joys of inter-personal communication through language (not to mention through bodily expression). I am a self-styled teacher and a believer in the intrinsic worth of knowledge. I am a lover and I love my wife and my family and I love myself.

But my substance ends there. My opaqueness ceases and the rest of me is qualitatively comprised of the same substance of which a schizophrenic is totally comprised. I refuse to fill up my glass void so quickly as do most people. It's a part of me and it changes daily as different light waves pass through it.

What alienates me from the rest of society is that I am actually perceived as being one with all consuming goals, meaning and direction, or as one who at least ought to have them. My true goal is to further my malleable chosen or acquired goals and beliefs and yet at the same time to affirm or at least defend the rights of my transparent void to coexist with my more socially acceptable stuff.

Now, about this book. It has elements of everything and nothingness at the same time. It deals with the finite nature of the potentially pathetic human existence on this earth and yet it also opens up our unstructured inner cores to allow us to expand and approach omnipotence and immortality. To realize that human beings in general, all of us, even the alleged super-stars of our society are frail, lonely, often pathetic creatures is to realize the beauty of the individual and his/her ability to come to grips with this void. It permits us to progress without filling ourselves up with mediocre top-soil, and to strangle the feelings of anguish that may from time to time creep in, when the void is flexing its muscles. If, as the existentialists say, we cannot know who we are nor from whence we came, how can we know what to do with our anguish? We can't I contend, so it seems best to kill it. AFFIRM THE VOID BUT KILL THAT DAMNED ANGUISH.

My book is a portrayal of our true human condition as perceived by our hero Martin P. Feinstein, an existentially based anti-hero. Marty's psycho-sexual development is traced, not through Freudian models, not through biological developments nor political theories, but rather through existential actions and occurrences.

The story of Martin P. Feinstein has three meshing phases although I wouldn't dare be so contrived and ordered as to suggest where one part ends and the next begins. We first find Marty rejecting society's filter for his void, affirming his inner nothingness and trying to "get off" on his suffering. As events transpire, he develops certain elements of substance that inextricably become a part of him. But his remaining void is still a powerfully existent voice from his past and it tells him to deny this phony substance and to re-affirm his total prior anguish.

In the final stage, Marty accepts his new findings but still retains his ductile void. But by incorporating the void he chooses to derive bliss and not feelings of human worthlessness and degradation. His accidental death is of little import in the end. Marty's life acquired meaning just by occurring. He wrestled down a plaguing philosophical knot, quite an accomplishment for any man or woman.

Martin's life is an optimistic existential working out of the truth, although one who is quick to read pessimism and desperate quietism into existential works could easily do so here. May I suggest to you that even if you can't get into Marty's head, get into his sexual fantasies and realities, his peaks and valleys, his travels and his friends. Existential framework or not, Marty's story is engaging.

You can look forward to hand jobs in a Varig jet, 36,000 feet above breathtaking Iguaçu Falls, oral stimulation administered to our fearless hero in his dilapidated Buick, and a sexual excursion with a woman older than Marty's maternal grandmother Emilia. On a more commonplace scale, you'll get an accurate picture of such attackable institutions as the pompous American dreamboat football jock, the big city publishing firm, the power elite's all women colleges, and in most lucid detail, the radio disc jockey, king of the advertising pimps.

Read and enjoy, and remember that any clever intertwinings in the plot, theme and character development

Richard V. Campagna

are purely coincidental, but for the symbolic pus pimple, which I'm putting you on notice to be sensitive to. The symbolism should be helpful to the reader, but absent that, I'm not here on earth to see if I can write a brilliant, tightly knit, symbolic work a là Charlie Dickens. I wish I could, quite frankly, but I probably can't and don't have the time to find out; so I figure I'm just here on earth to call reality as I see it, without catering to literary circles, academic elites and their analytical techniques.

Richard V. Campagna, Nov. 11, 2005

Chapter I

This is not a new beginning for me in life. There are never any new beginnings. I thought for a few slippery moments that I might have had one, but I now realize the utter inanity of such a thought. Life has only one beginning-when the pudgy ethnic doctor slaps your butt. It's got only one ending as well, and we never know for sure when it's coming or even when it's near. Right this very instant I'm sipping on some fairly decent coffee, being pretty suave and sensual in my mannerisms and fantasizing about balling one or two of the machinelike stewardii. They probably screw like machines too. But what a cool thing it'd be to get laid 28,000 feet above Virginia Beach.

I have no way of knowing what I'll be doing this evening. I may be having my muscles relaxed by a Brazilian masseuse and on the other hand I may be dead as a doornail (what's a doornail?), my mutilated skull with its tasty blood and chewy cerebral tissue serving as dinner for a school of inquisitive fish. I behave however, as though the latter more morbid possibility is absurd, even though it could take place. Roberto Clemente's soul can vouch for that.

I'm on my way to the lands of the Latins. Twenty-six

fascinating republics with political perspectives unimagined by the European monarchs and papal big shots when they first commanded and financed Latin American expeditions there some 500 years ago. I'm headed for Brazil (with a short stop-over in Caracas) to try and recover from the two brutal "emotional heart attacks" that have stained critically whatever pathetic excuse I previously had for felicity. For a while I also thought that such "heart attacks" could alter the structure of the soul. Clearly they don't. They merely whip it into newer and more encompassing frames of reference. The same soul is still with me that was with me before my sister died unexpectedly and before I had a chilling auto crash which reduced me to a puppet like android with fractured, dangling ribs and punctured, pleuritic lungs. I'm virtually totally recovered in the physical sphere, and at this juncture in time I'm working on my emotional comeback. In four hours time I'll be in South America, providing our pilot (mass-produced from Tiffen, Ohio) doesn't misguide this "bird" into the depths of the Caribbean. But what to do with my poor throbbing head? Where to discharge the confusion? I've got some direction now, but what honestly, the hell do I do with it? Isn't it just a phony meaning, springing from an underlying geyser of fear?

Who the hell do I think I am and why in the world do I think my life is of any import whatsoever? It's important mostly because I've got the cojones (vulgar in the Dominican Republic and elsewhere for "balls") to relate it openly and honestly in its nudest form. I refuse to couch my inner tragedy behind a piddling, pitiable shield of middle-class grooviness. I started this expose some months ago and I naively thought that my writing then was full of definite answers and viable game plans for peaceful living and for the maintenance of a revolutionary consciousness. I erred. I was a fool-as Rick Nelson says, "poor little fool." My writing then, and my existence then, as now, were only definable until some extraneous event beyond my control negated their worth.

My message today, which is as feeble as one's message can get, is that anyone's words are only valid for a fleeting moment in time. It seemed for a few days that there were some elements of substance in me-certain goals that weren't harnessed to my back by an over-indulging, brutalizing culture. Now I'm no longer sure.

I invite you to come back with me just a few short months. Join me inside my head, and if our industrious pilot doesn't screw up, and gets me to Brazil and environs and back, you'll get to read this work. If we go plummeting into a coral reef then my ideas will sink with me and you'll still be plagued with the dehumanizing myth that everyone must have a total definition—the kind that I don't have.

I'm gonna get some sleep now since it doesn't seem that any of the stewardesses have even cast me a glance. It's probably this round expanse of a pus pimple, flourishing underneath my left nostril. It's been there for a while but to pop it is beneath my dignity. It's part of me, it'll stay with me and if I don't get balled as a result thereof, I'll beat the proverbial meat.

In any event, read some of the dribble I've written during the past five months and get to know me a little better and I'll get back to you later on. Ciao!

Chapter II

BULLSHIT

By Martin P. Feinstein

Love is bullshit
Sharing is bullshit.
A share has as its only purpose
To bring gratification to its selfish initiator.
Kindness is bullshit
Consideration is bullshit.
Consideration never exists unless it is specifically returned.
Bullshit however, is just what is seems to be ... BULLSHIT!
Which is why BULLSHIT is the only thing that is not bullshit.

ZERO-SUM CONFLICT

Nobody has anything really important to say.

But if I just said that to you, you wouldn't believe me and you'd go ahead and read all those people who I claim have nothing provable to say.

So I'm forced to write an entire fucking book, telling you that neither I, nor a nybody else has any social treatise in which you should believe, be it on sex, love, social dynamics or politics.

I wish you'd all take a two month respite from reading and watching T.V. and think for yourselves....

And stop being duped by lies that writers and producers and poets invent and dress up to market like little piggies.

But you won't stop reading and watching the tubes. So if you have to read, read this! It's reading that tells you that nothing is worthy of being read.

1/25/73

I, Martin P. Feinstein find my head in a very strange state of affairs. Strange is not bad, mind you; strange is innovative. And so my head is in a state of innovation. To me, innovation is the excitement of being able to forget life's existential burden for any period of time and to undertake an adventure—an adventure self conceived and brought to fruition in the depths of one's own soul, with a bit of assistance from one's body perhaps.

I feel this way right now. Such a project as the one I am about to undertake will not answer the question of why I am living. Nor will it provide guidelines as to how I should conduct my life or even if I should continue to live.

Nothing can answer that. But my project will certainly make me forget, for some unpredictable time period, the omnipresent reality that I cannot now, nor will I ever be able to answer the three aforementioned perplexities. Yet if I can pursue my goal with the same vigor that now propels my pen I shall be content. I will have a purpose in spite of the fact that I have no purpose.

I intend to love a whore. That's right, a whore. Not merely an eighteen-year old Erasmus Hall High School sophomore whose promiscuity has earned her the reputation of being loose. Rather, my friends I'm going to love a woman who practices unlawful sexual intercourse for hire, in the exact manner proscribed by the New York State Penal Law. My woman is an attractive, capitalistically guided, street walking whore. I say that I will love her because I define love as being the act of loving someone and nothing more. If you are performing the acts of caring, consideration, communication and sexual union then let's face it—you're loving somebody. We haven't yet devised a force or a mechanism to qualitatively measure our emotions. Therefore, it matters not whom you are loving; it is only important that you are loving. And so, while I am presently loving others (my mother, and father, my brother and sisters, my dog Romeo and my rather odd excuses for friends), I will also begin to love my new friend, Jeanette, who just happens to be a hooker by profession. I already love her because I have decided to love her—and for no other reason. A friend of mine from college once wrote the following poem and for years now I've been dragging it around with me in my wallet along with a worn-out scum-bag. I never thought I'd be able to use it in my novel. He composed it for the first girl he ever balled and quite frankly it was a welcome change from his perverted limericks.

I—don't know you and I love you.

If I knew you for 100 years, would that make my love any stronger?

To love is merely the act of loving.

You don't know what's in my head

Nor I what's in yours.

Love is guesswork, love is goofing on the same thing

And above all

Love is fucking

And love is living together

And love is eating together

And leaving together

And coming together

And leaving together

And coming together.

I know I love you because I am in the act of loving you and for no other reason....

I think I agree with that horny old fool.

Getting back to my specific project, it's not so simple as it first appears. Not only do I want to offer my affection to Jeanette (the prostitute) in the most profound manner possible, but I want to offer her something that extends far beyond my insignificant affection. I yearn to offer Jeanette the opportunity to make some real choices in her life-choices that she herself is making because she herself wants to make them. These choices cannot be made walking the trash filled streets of downtown Brooklyn and catering to the whims of freaks, pimps, johns and junkies. Perhaps Jeanette chooses to remain on the streets. It may be of her own volition. But I suspect not. And so, accounting for this probability I am temporarily committing myself to corralling the means for my potential friend and lover to opt for a change.

I'm not totally crazy. Nor am I a literary genius, whatever that would mean. But admittedly I have a semi-hallucinogenic imagination and I do know how to tell a damn good story to any audience. Being so equipped, although she doesn't yet know it, I'm going to endeavor to record the developing love story of Jeanette and myself. Firstly I'm going to have to find her again, hope that she's got some sort of spine-tingling idiosyncrasy, and if not I must create one, to make my story have some rhythm.

To call my task cumbersome would be a gross understatement. After I relocate Jeanette I must tell her that I love her. I must explain that I love her because I want to love her and that since she is a human being she is needy and deserving of much love, as are we all. Whether or not she is married is of miniscule import. By the way whores get married too!

Anyhow, after I explain this rather unorthodox value plane to her I must then begin to explain that I would like to glorify her in words. I'll tell her that I believe her to be an exciting, sensitive, feeling person and that I'd like to offer her a chance to live as freely as I do. If she understands that I'm not putting her down, and that I'm not making any paternalistic value judgments, I will offer to give her half of the royalties from this book. In this way Jeanette can earn what she apparently needs most, without being forced to take to the streets. I'll further my

Richard V. Campagna

journalistic career by getting a book published and furthermore I'll meet another person; a person I would never have met had I used society's punitive guide book on inter-personal relations.

Who knows what cerebral waters percolate in Jeanette's head? Is she bitter, cynical, sarcastic, dull, perturbed, demented, frivolous, serious, tripped out? Is she taking smack, blowing dope, eating downs or does she have a very lucrative day time secretarial job with a super-understanding boss? Is she engaged in blissful wedlock, is she a mommy, a nomad, lonely, apathetic, dietetic or diabetic? Does she despise what she does or does she feel it to be little different from the absurd games that all of us play?

I know none of the answers to these queries and so reader, together you and I shall learn about the intricate trials and tribulations of my new love. I want to offer her my unconditional friendship and affection simply because she is a human being, experiencing life as she does and that's just as acceptable as any other life style. After all, unlike the construction of wood pipes, human development does not have an essence or a concept to follow. The life of Jeanette is her own, just like all of us have lives of our own. She's beautiful for that reason. And besides that, she's got succulent breasts. She must have the power to construct her own wood pipe.

Chapter III

I hold myself out as a partially spaced—out newsman on a small radio station in Providence, R.I. I don't bother with acid rock, underground suaveness or pop prattle. I don't even have my own show. My voice stinks in relation to the other DJs. I merely read the news on the hour and half hour. I live with my former college roommate, presently an engineer for a budding land-use planning firm outside of Boston. We eat together, get high together and from time to time take small road shows together, but as a rule I enjoy myself by myself, deriving most of my amusement from my own creative and intuitive processes. Physically, I've been told I'm very exciting, although if I'm parading on the beach with a group of friends you can be sure I won't be the first one noticed. Nor will I be the last. Although I'm rarely called handsome, the word "cute" is often tossed my way. I've also been termed as interesting, dynamic, romantic, sexy, foreign, far-out, Latin, intriguing, good looking and a host of other ridiculous but ego-strengthening adjectives. I've got long, brown, distinctively un-styled hair, pleasant features, free from distortion, a Sicilian nose and very dark, sensitive, pensive brown eyes couched in the shade of a bushy set of eye-brows. My forehead is broad, my hair line a trifle receding, my sideburns comically acceptable. My skin is quite dark for this Anglo-Saxon half of the hemisphere (Brazilians call it "Moreno"), and although it's not quite as clear as Mark Spitz's or David Cassidy's plastic-looking flesh, I like to think that the blemishes give a rugged effect. There's a rather conspicuous pussy looking whitehead beneath my left nostril. I always let it stay. Makes me feel super-human. All I can say is tough shit on the fools who don't get off on it. I'll not become a pimple picker for any one. Nor will I cover it with Clearisil. From now till eternity, the pimple and I are a unity.

I am virtually never cleanly shaven and often go three or four days without a shave, although that often results in oily, greasy skin. It's gotten to the point though, that I almost consider raunchy skin my philosophical companion. I supposedly became a Jewish man via the route of a Bar Mitzvah. I was born the product of an interfaith marriage which was governed by an agreement before the marriage (luckily not legally enforceable) to make me a nice Jewish kid. In reality, by faith, I consider myself existentially spiritual, cultivated in ethics alone. If God were to show himself to me just once, I would be the happiest person conceivable. After all, this would provide a meaning to my naked life. But as long as he remains locked up in other people's imaginations, I must conduct my life as if he were an amorphous force and I must wade through the froth of paradox and inconsistency alone and unsupported. I call this approach "optimistic existentialism".

While I don't believe that I can make it with every girl I see, I do believe that I have been blessed with an uncanny wit, intellect and artistry and a delightful rap which allow me to make any girl fall in love with my personality, my life style and my soul fairly easily. I don't know exactly where I obtained such power, nor can I specifically define it, but the more people I meet, the more I begin to believe in it.

I slouch at about 5' 10" and if I don my Brazilian boots I'm almost six feet. While I'm no king in the sport of arm wrestling, I have a remarkably strong back and chest and very powerful legs which are carryovers from my futile attempts at becoming a high school track star in order to get entry into an Ivy League School. I ran the half mile in 2:22.2 which was pretty shitty and I was forced to settle for Bucknell. It was there that I became a "Swiss cheese man" allowing my cheese-like frame to have each day's new reality breeze through its gaping holes. Amidst all the Muensters at Bucknell, this Swiss stood alone. Anyhow it seems that my "groovy" hairy thighs are a great advantage in my sophisticated powers of female acquisition. And I guess I'm pretty lucky to get so many women because I usually tire of them after very short periods of time. Except for one brief six month relationship in which I was totally dumped on my ass, I've never been in a typical boyfriend-girlfriend type set up. It's always seemed too contrived for me. I used to get fucked up about that, deeming myself to be some sort of inter-personal loser and weirdo, but I've come to realize that for me to call someone my girlfriend and keep a straight face I'd be molding myself, changing the natural physics of my mind and consequently eroding my spirit.

Most fascinating about my psycho-sexuality, at least to me, is that in addition to my romantically inclined female friends and diverse non-sexual companions, most of the real orgasmic excitement in my life is provided by "luscious" whores, "call girls" and mistresses. With them I can be me. I don't have to alter my thoughts, my actions and my grossness one iota. I concede, whores don't have the intellectual sensitivities that most of my Bucknell coeds have developed, but they do have a kind of mystique about them, a quickness, keenness, dynamicism and linguistic (note the pun) talent that adds a new dimension to my uncommitted life style. I'm not suggesting for one moment that a culture of whores and pimps is superior to a culture of academic discipline. I'm saying that whores are different from students and technically neither group is better or worse in this world of human individuals. Whatever man, woman, hooker or pimp does, has got to be right and correct. We know nothing of what we are, except that we are here, here to die. Our only values are, and can be that which our inner forces have eventually made us do. And that alone, the ultimate act, is what guides me.

I play my life pretty straight. I've got what society would call a primary girlfriend, one that trims my horns unconditionally except for the continued security with which I provide her. In addition I take out other assorted dishes. I attend occasionally, though decreasingly am able to tolerate, movies and rock concerts. I adore reading, writing and thinking and shooting hoops is fairly relaxing for me; even bowling can pass the time. But what truly turns me on is partaking in activities and assortments of values which are totally removed from my past. And so, when things are dull and draggy and pathetically bourgeois, I go and observe the whores in action. Only rarely do I purchase their services although on occasion I have been known to do so. But I enjoy watching these women, girls and in some cases virtual infants do whatever it is that they do to fill their own economic and personal gaps. To them a blow-job is like an hourly news report, a hand job, an A-Jax commercial.

And what's the big difference anyhow? Life itself makes us like tramps in a brothel. We prostitute ourselves to a philosophy, to a job, to a cause, to a cool demeanor and to a secure way out. We sell our souls to a definition. We are all whores, which in a sense mean that the street walkers are the only ones who spit right in reality's chubby-cheeked face. When they play their roles they assert how much they truly love and hate the market place. And even better, the hookers are cool; I love their boobs and asses and on a more hedonistic plane their raw sex totally flips me out.

What else about me might you like to know? Perhaps not much more. But if that's the case, then close the damn book. And if you wish to continue, and I assume you will, the breaks are with me, and since this is my book, I'll call the shots and set the tempo of behavior. I can tell you that I don't get hassled with money. I spend it as it comes and give it away just as fluidly. Some day I wish to make waves and improvements in this shit-hole world but for now I've been able to repress my childhood quests and I'm content just to hang out. And every so often, when I find my life restricted, contrived and buffoonish I immerse myself for two or three days straight into the mind-boggling intrigue of the culture of traditional degeneracy.

It helps me in convincing myself that what society labels "degenerate" values are no worse than the Ivy League values upon which I was nurtured. And when I understand this premise I can better understand that people who espouse values different from mine are no better or worse than myself-only different.

I've got a mother who still lives in Brooklyn's Flatbush section where I was born, where I spent 16 or so really intense years and where I go to visit four or five times per year. My mother likes me a real lot and she's a lot like me which probably explains how a 23 year old man can tolerate so much time with his "mommy." I saw "Floss" last week and initially I was not on a degeneracy spree. But life's activities don't always result in the same manner in which they were intended. It was then that I met Jeanette.

Chapter IV

I had called my mom and told her that I was coming home for a few days to check out some job opportunities and of course to see her for a belated Christmas, or in the alternative, an early Washington's Birthday. Anyhow it was late January. I had a pretty decent time at my childhood house in Brooklyn's competitive Midwood (Flatbush) section although my nights merely consisted of treks to Nathan's at Coney Island for $1.25 lobster rolls, a whirl on the Cyclone and three rye and gingers at the Midwood Lounge. When I say "Brooklyn's competitive Midwood section" I simply mean that whatever one tries to do in Brooklyn, some pushy person, with a neurotic competitive spirit (pretty good odds he's Jewish or Italian) is going to try to do it better than you, whether it's drive a car, buy a car, give a party, take a vacation, go to college or even have sexual relations. Luckily my short stays in Brooklyn don't place me on a collision course with any of these competition hungry assholes.

I had an interview with a New York-Boston publishing firm for a position as a manuscript reader and overall ombudsman for discontented authors and book retailers and I was virtually assured there would be a job opening for me within two months. I was pleased, Floss was happy for me and surely Cindy, my "primary" girlfriend would be happy. She'd been pretty down on Providence's social calendar and she longed for the chance to get to the "Big Apple." She was born in Augusta, Maine and although Providence was a step upwards for her with regard to size, its provinciality coupled with its "greasiness" really brought her down. Her father, a retired Air Force Colonel and a staunch WASP (y) ethnic racist Republican didn't teach Cindy too much about the advantages of our melting pot, pluralistic democracy; hence her contact with Providence's Italian, Polish, Portuguese and Puerto Rican communities was always distasteful and oftentimes repugnant to her. I was surprised she could even tolerate me, but perhaps my own snowballing spirits of anti-Zionism helped. In any event, I didn't see how the city was going to reduce her disdain for ethnicity's beauty-rather it would probably just drive our little stenographer further back into a Berkshire retreat. But she said she wanted to come with me to New York and we left it at that. Although I had suggested that she leave Pro country some time ago, she apparently had those old Laura Nyro wedding bell blues and did not want to lose her stultifying grasp on her closest vehicle to marriage-ME.

The afternoon during which I was planning to head back to Rhode Island, our Ocean State, the telephone suddenly rang. It was one of those quick rings that make you think there might not be another. But there was another. And another. And six others before I could lay down my suits and suede vests on my mother's fluffy bed and get to the receiver. It was Mr. Chasdi from the publishing company and he had the agonizing news that my position in the reading room was in jeopardy, double-jeopardy, but that a temporary quasi-janitorial slot was available in the interim. Was he fucking kidding? I really felt like telling him to shove a tuning fork up his ass; or as my brother Bobbie would say, suck on a hairy wang, but remembering that that would accomplish nothing I politely hung up. It takes setbacks like that to get my cerebral waters percolating and this reversal of fortune was no exception. The chain reaction of thoughts began to utilize my cranium as an indoor trampoline and squash court and from a simple job rejection, in a matter of minutes, I was involved in the thick of an existential crisis. I alluded to them earlier, but let me re-paint the picture a bit more specifically.

As a rule I carry on my life with a minimum of emotional energy stress. But when my inane pragmatic goals leave me short of fulfillment or when I don't behave or appear the way I'd like to, or the way I want others to see me, due to my inability to fully determine my life, I commence a process that I term "weirding out." I do so in a very strange and psychotically frightening way. I start to realize that I have no models to follow, and that there are no men or woman in contemporary America worthy of emulation. The country is made up of either money men, jocks, fascists or freaked out paupers. And the truly kind people, the unassuming compassionate souls are increasingly locked away in fortresses of anonymity while the obnoxious pigs pollute the air with their stardom oriented rhetoric. During such dilemmas of my soul, my responsibility is placed squarely on my back, like an eternal chicken fight, and I can't look to God or to my mommy or to my girlfriend for an answer. I temporarily acquire a monstrous burden and have no place to put it. The more I think, the more complex my cycle gets until I feel like a total schizoid man in total despair. The only way to end the cerebral bombarding and resultant psychological torture is to fall out or smoke some hash. When I awaken I usually remember the presence of the unanswerable questions but

I can better understand and digest the fact that they can never be answered by anybody. And so I try to carry on as before-a little more weary, but a trifle stronger at the same time.

And so after my little exchange of words with Simon Chasdi, I went into a three hour wrestling match with "transient schizophrenia" on my mother's multi-cushioned purple couch and eventually fell asleep until 8:30 that evening. Flo was out with some friends of hers on the Avenue for some Chinese food and wouldn't be back until 11:30. My brother Bobbie was at a friend's for the night, working on a school political campaign, my sister Denise combing Kings Highway for the perfect pair of Clogs and my sister Andrea, 18, away enjoying the independence of her freshman year at the University of Wisconsin in Madison. Rather than hassling the whole thing out with Flossie, and rather than re-explaining to her the ultimate absurdity of my life, I decided I'd just split and leave her one of my brutally tender notes of affection. Brutal in the sense that my affection attempts parallel those of Henry Kissinger; honest in their intent but blurred in the delivery somehow. I knew that after I put away some Chock Full of Nuts coffee at the junction and an egg creme at Bamboo Lew's on Parkside, a couple of packs of weeds and a long car ride with some soothing Jim Croce tunes, my dilemma would be resolved anew, synthesized with the rest of my head, at least for a couple of months.

Into my '63 Buick Wildcat and down the crumbling, sloppily tarred bumpy thoroughfare called Ocean Avenue. Running red lights like a lunatic, I got to Church Avenue and was preparing to turn left to approach the Prospect Expressway. Out of nowhere a tall, thin black girl, with a great looking Afro darted in front of my car and caused me to come to a screeching stop, complete with whirling skid. The stop made me look so clownish that I instinctively dug my own ostrich hole by putting my head down as if I were trying to adjust my emergency brake and when the light still refused to change I picked up the copy of the Village Voice on the seat and virtually wrapped it around my head. The black chick didn't even turn around but just kept on running, clutching onto her cassette player and comb.

I lit up another Parliament and immediately as if an S.O.S. were sent down my spine, it dawned on me that I had barely missed thrashing to death a girl who was a virtual cross between Melba Moore and Teresa Graves. She was so fuckin' beautiful I couldn't control myself. And with my imagination and sexually predisposed mind I soon projected onto the movie screen inside my skull thousands of split second images which depicted the remarkable sex appeal of our Afro-American women especially to little Portnoys like me. And if you haven't already guessed, my rather unorthodox value and thought plane brought me to an immediate analysis of the black and Puerto Rican prostitute collection that congregates in Brooklyn's downtown area. My mind flashed back to my last experience with these lovely maidens about nine months ago and just as the light changed I knew that once again it was time to relieve my head of the burdens of middle classdom and submerge into the life of sleaziness. I didn't have the usual three days to devote to this "vacation" so I knew I was to have a one niter. But I would make it good. And it would help me to demean the importance of a good job and to shrug off the remains of my existential trauma. I corrected my semi-turn and hit the gas pedal forcefully, lifting my spirits, virtually lifting my tires off the black top and heading straight on to the raunch palace of the world-downtown Brooklyn.

As I continued down Ocean Avenue, visions of deli-cious black, and sun bronzed white women danced across my window in between the pigeon shit and soot. Tall slen-der ones, short stocky ones, ones with long straightened hair, ones with giant afros and ones with amazingly bizarre make-up. All of my fantasy women had large, almost monstrous breasts and nipples and huge, protrud-ing, accentuated buttocks. Their succulent, moist, smooth lips and sensual thighs assaulted my imagination and somehow my brain transferred the message to my foot which was soon flooring the accelerator. Then I began to imagine voices. Deep, hoarse, calculating voices with a powerful mixture of a Brooklyn accent and a southern Biloxi Mississippi drawl. I was in a total frenzy. And then of course I imagined the sexual act. It didn't seem dirty, it didn't seem immoral and it didn't seem fucked up. It seemed pleasant and it was going to be professional and most importantly it was going to satisfy me at that point. And I knew I wanted it then. Another traffic light and the incredibly complex illusions continued. Five and six black women attacking my body from all angles with techniques borrowed from Fellini and Linda Lovelace. Up the ass, down my legs and virtually encircling my balls were long, mobile, juicy tongues. These women, by their actions and by their being were going to make me happy. Simon Chasdi was not. Who should I desire more? The cretin publisher or a whore? Who was worthy of more respect? Chasdi couldn't pull out a draw if he gave me the key to the drafting room.

That was it. No more time for thinking. The time had come. I was on the corner of Flatbush Avenue and Pacific Street and as I made the left turn I could see lurking against the delapidated brownstones, the highly coveted sexual meat. Some of the candidates were leaning against buildings, some were strolling down Pacific Street scratching their private areas and others were proudly situated on the corner, blowing imaginary bubbles and pulling up their stockings. All were dressed in traditionally tuff garb, ranging from tight fitting hot pants (I guess they all fit tight), to amazingly short skirts, to dungaree bells. Between Flatbush Avenue and 4th Avenue there must have been nine or ten girls (our experts tell us between the ages of 13 and 49), smacking their lips, wiggling their snake-like tongues, spreading their legs, and the most creative ones even grinding their midsections against parking meters and above fire hydrants. Sensuality in its rawest and most natural form and I don't mind saying that I soon contracted a partial hard-on. I slowed down, and as each saw my brake lights flicker, each girl in turn stopped in her tracks and gave that old college try in order to summon me to her side. Each flashed her face at me and then beckoned me with her best sensuality trick. Even a 6'2" transvestite seemed to want a piece of my action. And although at that point I welcomed the chance to attack any one of them, I had only $15 to spare and I didn't want to blow it. I continued down Pacific Street to an even roguier section, totally excited and somewhat strung out.

I passed one total pig, a white chick with scar tissue and blackheads posing as her face and with hair as shaggy as un-cleaned wool still on the lamb. I slowed down again, only to find three guys, apparently, from the isle of Puerto Rico pitching quarters in an alley way. And then, out of the clear, or rather dark blue sky, an amazing vision turned the corner and stood herself right against a broken parking meter. I knew she wasn't a meter maid. But was she a hooker or a stewardess? Perhaps both. She was Jeanette.

The red VIOLATION sign loomed in between her long, attractive fingers. The woman was spectacular.

Two cars passed her in front of me and she made no attempt to flag them down. She merely stood there. And with her simple and knowing smile looked straight across the street at a billboard of Stiller and Meara fighting over a bottle of Blue Nun wine and a lobster. She had straight, shiny hair, not at all greased down and very possibly a fall. She had the most appealing face I believe I have ever seen. Her skin was light brown, her lips were marblelike; not too thick, but firm and active looking. She had a perfect nose and big, circular, magnetic brown eyes, adorned with only a minimal amount of eye make-up. She stood about 5'5" and was solidly thin if you know what I mean. Yet she sported a tantalizing pair of breasts. She smiled amicably in my direction but that was all. No grinding, humping, leg spreads, no opened buttons or zippers and no sexual acrobatics of any sort. Clearly, I wanted a better chance to look at her but this time I made the light and was forced to turn the corner. Consequently I had to circle the block, since you don't just pull over, park and stroll calmly around downtown Brooklyn at night unless you're a Panther, a junkie, a cop, a judo expert or a lunatic. I was in an outrageous state of mind although it was no longer a sexual frenzy alone. It was an emotional frenzy-an emotional volcano was bubbling inside of me. I had to get to that girl, even if just to tell her that her prices were too expensive. I had to hear her voice and see what she was like. She appeared to be the sweetest girl I had ever seen and I never use that word.

I slammed my foot on the gas, but as I got back to 4th Avenue I missed another light. I was afraid that someone would "snatch" her up at any minute and that I would lose my second chance at beholding her magnificence. I was right. When I returned to her spot she was gone and in her place was a buxom, powerful Puerto Rican momma, apparently broaching the forty year mark, who would have done the trick any other nite but that one. She was sexy, in her own bizarre style but she couldn't even come close to exuding the emotional magnetism of the girl who was to be called Jeanette.

I circled the block seven times and had promised myself that after ten circuits I would abandon my "project" as soon as practicable by getting blown by the first slut in sight and heading up to Providence. Sure enough on the ninth round-tripper Jeanette was back and I wasn't taking any chances. She cast me a glance which led me to believe that she recognized my face or at least my jalopy, so I hit the non-power brakes and pulled over to her curb. She approached slowly, probably fearful of pigs and other insidious characters, and I leaned over to lower my window.

"How much for a blow?" I politely inquired.

"Five dollars. And for ten I'll lick around the balls."

"O.K. Ten is fine."

Jeanette smiled and got in. I never have trouble with strangers; whores or otherwise. I told you before that I can make almost any girl dig my soul. I don't care if they're Spanish, French, Bajan or Swedish. And Jeanette, I hoped, would be no exception. And she had to dig my body, or at least pretend to 'cause that's what she was getting compensated for.

"Boy it's warm in here. This is the warmest car I've been in all night."

"Gee, that's funny; the heat is on low. When I put it on high you feel like you're on the Equator. But I guess it's pretty nippy out there." Dead Silence.

Jeanette grabbed my thigh and said, "By the way honey, you're really cute and I like you."

Then she formally introduced herself as Jeanette Thompson from Bedford-Stuyvesant, the super-ghetto of Brooklyn, known to its natives as Bed-Stuy.

I said that I'd been born and raised in Brooklyn but that I really didn't know exactly where that area began and ended. She proceeded to explain and I realized that I actually did know. I told her my name was Marty and that I was on my way up to Providence.

"Marty honey, how old are you? I saw you drive by the first time about twenty minutes ago and you looked 16 or 17."

I was confused. I was complimented that she recognized me through the car window but I was not exactly thrilled that I was giving off vibrations of being six years younger than I really was.

"I'm 23," I said. "And that's surprising that I look young to you. I don't often shave and when that's the case people often take me for 24 or 25. How old are you? 19?"

"No, I'm 26. But people usually say that I look really young. Do you think I look that young?"

"Yup! At least younger than I do."

Jeanette told me to take the next right and two quick lefts. We were on Butler Avenue behind an old dilapidated truck and I swear there wasn't one light on the street. I turned out my headlights and shut off the motor as per standard, "whore chasing procedure." There was an old man in a tattered Army jacket with Jerry Garcia's picture on it, and to combat the nippiness in the air this old dude was apparently masturbating across the street. But he couldn't even get it together enough to get an erection, no less hassle us. How did I know he couldn't get hard? I was looking.

I didn't really want a blow job. I wanted to look at Jeanette and I wanted to talk to her and I wanted to kiss her. But how could I tell her that? So, I prepared to accept her mouth. I paid her the $10 bucks first, and gave her a shiny quarter as well, complying with something I'd read in the book THE FOLKLORE OF PROSTITUTION. My pants unzipped and loosened I was ready to go.

"I'm comin' to you baby," she moaned.

And she came to me. And boy it was good. I'd been to a whore only once in my life for oral stimulation five years ago in Amsterdam. After Jeanette's rendition it was as if I'd never been before. Her style was inimitable. She spent about two minutes on foreplay, which is pretty unique in the "privacy" of one's own car, and if you can believe it, she made me come for 15 or 20 seconds. I pumped out my spermatazoa as if I were one of Jed Clampett's oil wells. The whole process was just too enjoyable for me to ruin it by attempting to record it with my inadequate words and paltry phrases. Use your imagination.

The strange part of the matter was that I actually felt as though Jeanette were enjoying it. I'd swear to it. I honestly felt as though she had an emotional commitment to make me happy. It was as if she really wanted me to be satisfied. I'll probably be proven to be the most naive newsman in the history of broadcasting. But I'd stake my reputation on the girl's sincerity.

That's all I know of Jeanette right now. She blew me in the front seat of my car. I've seen her for a total of twenty minutes. On the ride back to her station we talked about cars, my education, Hank Aaron, Providence, Boston, inner city pigs (cops) and their personalities and Puerto Ricans. Nothing very heavy. Just about things. She had a flair about her. She was exciting, fresh, appeared to be clean (for my organ's sake), pretty, mature and different as all hell. And she was living.

"Well Marty, it was my pleasure meetin' you. I really do hope I see you again soon, O.K.?"

"Be good Jeanette," I said. And I grabbed her arm and kissed her.

That was it ...

Chapter V

I'm tired and atypically beat, a short two weeks back in Providence after my encounter with Jeanette. I'm still shipping Cindy around as if she were a chunk of chuck steak. She's not even a good fuck any more. She's clumsy as hell and orally she was always a loser. Always getting her goddamn teeth where they shouldn't be. We're seeing movies, going to Celtic games and cursing out Dave Cowens, and from time to time we even do up one of the Valle's Steak Houses in the greater Rhode Island area. But I'm bored as shit. I'm not in anguish and I'm content with my "absurdity" for the time being, but I've still got a neurotic itch to bring my project to fruition or at least to a definitive closing. What makes this project fascinating is that it's my own creation—it's not someone else's trip with a slight little twist. It's my own project, based upon my own design and desires. And my ultimate desire, my temporary void-filling goal is to be good to Jeanette.

Why Jeanette and not Cindy? Why Jeanette and not my mother? Why Jeanette and not myself? Jeanette because—Jeanette is different. And Jeanette because Jeanette needs assistance in being her true self. And Jeanette because Jeanette is being pushed into commitments that she'd probably prefer to hold off. And Jeanette

Richard V. Campagna

because why not Jeanette?

I can't think of much else besides her. I've temporarily lost all semblance of emotional normalcy. I don't give a flying shit about my newscasts. I don't really give a damn about Cindy. For all I care she can go pick strawberries on her Uncle's farm. I have a chance to invent a totally bizarre project that would totally flip out everyone around me if they only knew. But they don't know nor are they capable of discerning what's happening in my mind and thus they treat me as usual-they treat me as a "darling, sweet boy who's searching for his true identity and who's struggling to make it in the radio world." Yet if this account of my thoughts were to be made public I would be totally ostracized from the "civilized" world. How stupid are people? How contradictory and foolish are they? Screw 'em though. I've got a chance to give feigned meaning to my life through this ludicrous exploration and conquest and I'm not going to be denied.

Morty Gelfand at the station told me that something was lacking my voice. He said that I should put some concern into it. How could I Morton? I'm not really concerned about Cyprus or Lebanon or Londonderry.

So while I continue to hang out in my three room apartment with Jackie, I go through days at a time saying fewer than a hundred words to the people with whom I work. All I want to do is write a book about a fantasized love affair with Jeanette, an exalted hooker, and at the same time show untested and unconditional affection to another human being that I know nothing about. I don't think I'm crazy. I'm merely what's come to be known as the sane-schizoid personality of our time. It's a beautiful feeling. But I'm always on guard to counter unfounded charges of lunacy. It's me against four billion others. I'm just different.

At night I stuff my ears with John Coltrane, Boz Scaggs, Poco and some strange pianist I came across, Carol Hall. And I think. I don't need Cindy or any pathetic, patchwork excuse for a girlfriend. I want to see Jeanette, and if I can fulfill my imagination then I can prove that I have real control over my destiny. The power to get to know someone who by society's standards I should have no business knowing, can become mine. This far out relationship will be a victory over society's stagnancy. The fact that I, Marty Feinstein, a total nebbish up until grade eleven, raised on borscht and gefilte fish, could break into the ghettos of South Brooklyn, pick up a voluptuous black hooker and subsequently cause her to care for me, would give me a feeling of potency. Potency of the soul. I'm a man of action and my passion is unbridled.

I often picture Jeanette's luscious body entangled with mine in my mahogany framed, brass-backed double bed. Our bodies make a perfect fit. In my dream she's constantly kissing me with her amazingly soft lips and passionate tongue. And she just sits and lies for hours at a time and asks me questions about life and I ask her the same ones. And our answers are remarkably the same. Although our acculturization processes were 180° apart, our analyses of our "one life" situation are precisely congruous. An so, in my imagination we lie together and make love and space out and come down and flow with soft rock music and wait for something to get our asses in gear. If it doesn't come along just right, we'll keep on balling. And so go my dreams. Both in the daytime and at night.

I know I want to love Jeanette. That's all I want for now. It's one of those intuitive thought processes upon which I base my life. And this is one upon which I feel commanded to follow up. I must return to the scene of my blow job and tell Jeanette that I love her and that I cannot resist her captivating face nor her meaningful body. I must tell her that if she wants I will write a dynamic, expository novel about the feelings and values of a professional prostitute and that I believe it will sell. And I repeat. I will offer her half the royalties to help provide her with a chance to leave the streets.

What if she wants no part of my nonsense? What if she's married? She is 26. What if she totally freaks out and thinks I'm trying to expose her miserable existence? What if she thinks I'm a cop? The more these questions begin to build the more I know that this imaginary plot is not confined to my imaginatory processes. It's a real desire and it's incessantly seeking expression. Even if I fail, I've got an interesting short story for publication. And right now I'm powerless to resist. That mental force that makes me despise conformity and order is commanding my ego. The unbelievable, the unheard of, the ridiculous, the inane and the sleazy are my most cherished goals of existence.

Jeanette told me that she usually comes out on Monday nights about 11:30. I can't risk the bothersome and time consuming drive to the city and the shitty food on the Connecticut Turnpike only to find out that she's not out. So it'll have to be on a Monday night at 11:30 when I make my next attempted encounter with my love.

I don't know her address, her telephone number nor any of her friends so the only thing for me to do to make contact is to find her on the streets. I'll have to go to the place where I beheld her the last time. Most hookers stay in one specific area—they like to keep on their own turf to get a better understanding of their clientele and of the police routes.

My next trip to New York City will be two weeks from this Monday night. My last show is 6:30 so I've got five hours to get to Brooklyn. I can probably eat at one of the putrid Nutmeg Inns on the way to break up the journey.

I've got concern back in my voice according to Morty. I know it's not due to a Papal declaration or Jimmie Hoffa's release from prison but its concern just the same and it'll keep me from getting the boot from work. I've been saying more to the people at work these past two days. It's probably because people bother me less and less as my project takes up more and more of my time. I now have meaning. I have ambition, I've got adventure and I've got guts. And I'm assured of my individuality since I know that no one else in the world is thinking what I'm thinking.

Chapter VI

My head began to get weird like it is now at Bucknell University in Lewisburg, Pa., as I finally got myself reasonably together during my last two years. Yup, I guess I'm a pretty bright kid. Society would say to me, "You're a bright boy, with wit and ambition. Don't have anything to do with slutty pigs; girls who are beneath you. Get married and be a good solid member of society. Earn your way." It's to combat such logical dogma that I must do what I'm about to do. I can't let any definition as to how a good person should act, guide me. I must make up my own itinerary. And I must show the world that I remain good in spite of my dubious acts of "perversion." I must show that I am kind and peaceful and that I can help all people instead of tossing them off as vagrants. And my attainment of confused, almost maniacal levels is to assure myself that I am my own master, with myself alone to answer to, with a little guidance perhaps from my "maker."

People would probably call me paranoid if they knew me well. But to show them how stupid they are, I behave secretly and offer them a totally false impression of myself—a milk-toast radio personality. And as I continue to be strange, mixed-up and unsure of myself, the idiots who would be the first to have me locked up don't even know who I am or what I really stand for.

I am a man of no pre-ordained concepts. This leaves me a totally malleable figure ready for every twist of fate. By living in such a way I can then become the ordered, structured society man at any time. Right this instant I could get married, have two smiling, ruddy cheeked kids and cop liberal political and platonic philosophical ideas. But once I do that I'd be dead inside.

That day can always come. My days with Jeanette cannot. That is why I am the way I am. It gives me internal excitement and keeps me bouncing along. My mind never stops, my imagination never ceases. Each night I dream about my whisperings with Jeanette. And I make love to her in the depths of my mind. She doesn't have to do a thing. Her soul is omnipresent. I just keep painting beautiful slides in my head; quick flashing slides of Jeanette and me twisting and turning nakedly on Providence's fashionable East side lawns and fountain studded parks, away from the repugnant dark streets of Brooklyn and away from her death dealing amigos.

The confidence with which I undertake my task stems from my past experience and successes in influencing people and also from a possible misconception that Jeanette might have. She may, in a misguided system of logic, feel that I am above her station in life, intellectually and financially. But if this tool (the fact that I have supposed class, money and education) works, I will destroy it as a weapon, making Jeanette my absolute equal, something I earnestly believe she is.

Only eight days to go until New York. The pleasure is like a lethargic form of intercourse. Speaking of intercourse and the lack thereof, I have begun to masturbate recently. Only to the thought of Jeanette, though.

If I fail miserably in my endeavor, I'll probably just invent another one. But I don't give up easily and I don't believe I'll fail, at least on the merits of my own case. Yet sadly enough, there are extraneous circumstances and dangers completely beyond my control that could shoot holes through the entire set of plans I've concocted, i.e. getting rolled by one of Jeanette's lovable pimps, or getting arrested by one of New York's finest for illicit intercourse or even getting circumstantially involved in a drug bust.

Please pray for Jeanette and me. You'll hear from me soon after the battle. The victory will be when I assimilate Jeanette's soul and values into mine, creating a love-sharing relationship that also allows each of us to submerge in and out of each other, at will.

Chapter VII

I met death yesterday. He or she, or whatever sex it is, is no big deal. I hit a bump on a highway and was virtually catapulted into a deathlike trance. My body totally meshed with the universe, my mind expanded a million fold as well. I never lost consciousness; rather it seemed as though I'd tripled what I had. Aware, happy, content, alive was I. Nothing to fear, no big sweat and it didn't matter one fuckin' bit that in life my name never made it into lights or that I'd not yet born a little urchin. There was nobody to listen to or to care about what I'd done on earth. And there was nothing to keep me from enjoying myself totally. Only human psychological distrust of the unknown and the unproven keeps mankind from a very enjoyable part of life, that is, death.

Richard V. Campagna

Chapter VIII

I screwed it up. And I mean royally. It's over and done with. Here are the gory details of the losing encounter.

I had a quick rush of dates before the New York sojourn and only for one was I able to get an erection. The girls all really sucked, not literally. And the one for which I was able to get hard wouldn't have sex with me. She had some hysterical monotonous rap on morality which I quickly shut out by calling Chubbie's Cab Service to take her home. I stuffed a five spot in her pocket for the tip. Cindy is just horrible and she is out of my life forever.

Anyhow, all that shit didn't matter since I was to see Jeanette in two days. Before I left I thought to myself, "Marty, you're sick. You're really sick." I didn't care.

However my delicate tower of bizarre building blocks came tumbling down pretty heavily. What a horror show my second encounter with Jeanette turned out to be. She didn't even know that I inhabited the earth. I drove five hours to have her tell me that her sacred blow jobs had risen from $10 to $12. She didn't even know who I was at first. She passed me off as another horny customer and in fact mistook my ethnicity for that of a native of Boca Chica.

"Qué te pasa?"

"Uh, how much for a blow?"

"Twelve dollars tonight, you going out?"

"O.K.," I said, hoping and still truly believing that this would be the last blow job to cost me money. Dead silence again. Jeanette was in an incredibly bitchy mood.

"Do you remember me?" I offered.

"Yeah, you been down around here before."

Thanks a million baby, I thought to myself.

How the hell could I tell this chick that I love her? How could I begin to explain values, freedom, being or existence to her? How could I even say anything to her? She wants to suck and fuck and beat on schmuck and get paid for it and apparently nothing else. Her work however is superb. I let her do me up once more.

She licks around the testicles and then works her tongue up the erect penis, all without the use of the lips. Then, as the tingling sensation begins to spread, almost like a shot of Novacaine, she devours the tip of your penis with her voluptuous lips and begins to moisten it. Then up and down, furiously about ten or twelve times before orgasm and then she sucks out the entire emission before she's through. Almost a vacuum-like experience—you feel drained, relieved and ready to go again, to keep being sucked along life's path. And what's miraculous is that there ain't one solitary sperm on your B.V.Ds. Truly an exhilarating experience.

But I was in anguish. My dreams were in shambles. I saw myself as I was back in the 10th grade. A punky, schmucky middle class asshole, totally drained after ejaculation and with nothing to show for it. I was sick of myself, my activities and most of all my miserable failure and absurd fantasies; and I wasn't even close to communicating with Jeanette.

I just wanted to be by myself. I couldn't look at Jeanette so I whipped her back to her station on Pacific Street. I was undeniably alone. The total horror of the world could have found refuge in my soul at that moment in time. And I couldn't get my confidence back by merely picking up a whore because a whore had just torn it to shreds.

But it wasn't sexual confidence I had lost. It was communicative, emotional confidence that was seemingly gone and I had to regain faith in myself. Faith that I was charming, inspiring and overpowering to a degree. Only two girls in the world could have gotten my life blood circulating again and one of them, my sister Andrea was 1,100 miles away.

Fortunately, the other happened to have a cubicle on 112th Street and Amsterdam Avenue in New York, near the ever popular Hungarian Pastry Shop. The girl's name was Marla Swenson and she was an old co-ed friend of mine from Bucknell. I had to see her and I headed for that Flatbush Avenue Extension to the Manhattan Bridge across to the West Side Highway and zoomed uptown. This time I was surer than ever I'd bypass the hookers in front of Nathan's on 43rd Street.

Chapter IX

2/9/71 – A Marty Feinstein to Marla Swenson letter while both were still at Bucknell/Topic: Marty's neurotic need for a girlfriend, somewhat disguised.

Dear Marla,

At this juncture in the new and enlightened semester, namely the first day of classes, I thought it would be appropriate to fill you in on a couple of thoughts of mine that seem to have transcended our most recent conversation. Before I begin let me add that I just packed away 250 pages of Rollo May's LOVE AND WILL in my inimitable one—sitting fashion and the urge hit me to get into your head. For your eyes' sake and for your ultimate convenience I decided to give my wrists a workout; hence this typewritten letter.

After a powerful and all-encompassing semester of "existential anguish" which seems to have rocked the hearts and souls of those near and dear to me (including myself and excepting you) I believe it is desirable to be stronger than the anguish and use it as one's tool.

It appears that right now I'm at a very content and honest stage in my existence. In the past, as I lived my

Richard V. Campagna

traditional mode, I carried along with me a variegated collection of cover-ups and disguises and masquerades that draped and often obscured or even warped my true self. Although this masquerade tended to convey my personality in a very adorable, likeable, personable and take charge form, what was truly underneath seemed only to make its way to the surface on rare occasions, and even then only very haphazardly. It was always forced to submerge beneath a deluge of societal forces. I knew all along and very intimately this true identity and I knew that it wasn't getting the work out that it deserved. I believe that you were also pretty well acquainted with this flabby, amorphous creature that you often met on the sly, beneath the Ivy League roles that it had been playing. But neither of us openly heard from my real self as society tried to mangle it beneath the guise of academic achievement, chicks with tight asses and a big, yapping mouth.

It took an eighteen-year-old girl whose love I question at this point and a little guts meshed with a lot of pain to bring out my other bedfellow again. So now, my real self seems to be working steadily and doesn't want to go back on welfare again. In fact, I believe I'll give him a no-cut contract. And the beautiful part of the whole situation is that he (this new personality of mine) is able to coexist with the very being and the very society that shackled him for so long.

If this isn't clear to you (which I'm sure it is) I'll rephrase my thoughts in one more way. What I've been doing has been playing inter-personal chess (in the Hessian conception of the word) for twenty years with some pretty fancy pieces and moves and yet I was missing my Queen. I kept rearranging my pieces but was missing the essential element of my attack. Now I've recaptured the biggest and best piece of all—my true self. And I plan to do some heavy rearranging for the next sixty years or so, unless some enemy driver nips my life in the bud.

If you haven't yet guessed, this letter is, in its own sort of way, a thank you note for sub-consciously understanding my "queen" even though she wasn't predominant in my personality. Thank you for understanding it and for loving it. There are very few people who ever met it and you're one of them. You've been able to capture my nature without the aids of rational-emotive therapy, Yoga, encounter groups, transactional analyses or psychedelic use.

As I try to reciprocate this process in understanding you, I note similar themes that recur. I have a feeling about your chubby little innards that seems to be hidden even to some of your closest friends and my second purpose in writing this letter is to let you know that I have a bead on it. If I'm mistaken and the above is not really sensible to you, I'd like to know about it in letter form. O.K.? I'll be cooling it on the philosophical plane for now, so let me lapse into the bourgeois trivia that envelops our existences.

My courses should be really good this time around in the respect that they're easy, they offer enjoyable reading and I'll get plenty of opportunities to shoot off my mouth in the seminars. My free days, Tuesday, Thursday and Friday should be great for fucking off, hanging out, weirding out, shooting hoops, driving around in the death-mobile and just meeting people. Also, I'll be able to do a little more writing and a lot less bullshitting with the somewhat played out Bucknell preppies.

Roommate Pete just came bombing in, back from a delightful weekend baking apple pies with Rosalie. As straight as that mother-fucker is, I'm really looking forward to a dynamite semester with his revamped attitudes on political liberalism, drugs and women. Am dropping my independent study on the Philosophy of Laura Nyro and instead and in lieu of that one, am taking a course on that tortured Spanish existentialist, Miguel de Unamuno. But remember, like I already told you, the anguish is not my value but rather my implement and pulley to liberate me from society's bullshit.

Finally, thanks for the dinner last week. I really get off on your friends, but as a self-respecting male I can't keep coming to see you all in a coffee-klatch type set up and gab about clothes, fashion, music and your belated periods. I enjoy talking to all of you, but it can't really continue as it has been. I feel like a foppy little fart. Like a goofy little shit. Like a goddamn ding-a-ling. It's for this reason that you'll have to come to my place, or in the alternative I could see people individually. Any basis will do; friend, date, ping pong partner.

I'm pretty happy with this letter and I hope it's clear and positively received. It's written from the heart and I hope I've expressed the strong feelings that I have for you. If you misread me I'll break your slender behind. Now to drop dead from a wrist attack.

Love,

MARTY

Chapter X

Back to the brutal present, bouncing off the cushion of the past—My encounter with Maria after the disaster with Jeanette.

Maria had put on about 15 pounds since the last time I'd seen her. We went out for a while during my freshman year at Bucknell; she was still a coed at Dickinson in Carlyle, PA and transferred to Bucknell as a junior. Ever since I'd known the old goat her weight and personality were so erratic that I could never get into her for any length of time. Marla was the first chick ever to show me that what I thought might be affection was in effect bullshit. I never really cared for Marla except for the fact that I wanted her to love and admire my ass and in reality I used to pay more attention to her roommates and friends and sisters than I did to her. But through her I learned that in spite of the fact that I was a prick at heart, I could still understand my prickiness and quixotically attempt to be a real human being, somewhat helpful to others.

Marla had given up she told me. She never knew who she was, where she belonged or with whom she should hang out. She was of Swedish descent but atypically fat, lazy, up-tight, middle class and dull. I always wanted to have her natural kindness without her natural dullness. When I arrived at her Amsterdam Avenue pad, paid for by her Swedish sociologist daddy, I let her speak first. It would relax my head, put me into a new frame of mind and give me time to organize my thoughts.

"Marty," she said, "I'm really fed up with myself. I left Bucknell without a personality and I still haven't conjured up one. I knew that Brillo (her boyfriend) wasn't right for me and rather than submerge, I'm stuck here alone at NYU studying the most crippling social science of all: boring, bullshit academic anthro. I'm really fucked up.

"I keep getting fatter and fatter and the more I eat, the more I have to eat to reduce my self-consciousness in public places. And it's the same with my beer drinking, as this disgusting belly shows. (She grabs an enormously disgusting chunk of her pot belly and grunts a few times) I have no dates and yet I couldn't bear to fuck for any of those greasy tweeds that pinch my ass in bars.

"Marty, my problem is that I've got the desires and hopes of a dynamic, beautiful Jewish American princess from Woodmere and the body of an overweight Argentinian tortuga. If I wasn't so cool it wouldn't be as distasteful, but I am cool and I'm eternally aware of the fact that I can't even come close to attaining what I feel I deserve."

I always had an amazing compassion for over-weight, unattractive girls because unlike guys, a girl can rarely get around it. Guys with weird noses or frizzy hair or fat asses or pot bellies can often convert those physical oddities into something of a personality novelty and sense of humor. If a guy can develop an air of coolness or cockiness or cuteness about him he's in there with all sorts of good looking babes. No such luck for females. Unattractive girls are virtually doomed to a life of vicarious living. And even your most open-minded intellectual being won't tell you much different. Even friendships with such women don't last and I've found that there's no use kidding myself. What it boils down to is that if we really wanted to help all people live more fulfilled lives we'd lift more faces and ass flab instead of mass producing missiles. And anyhow, changing faces is a lot easier than changing millions of infected minds. It shouldn't be this way, but it is.

Marla was really getting intense about the doomsday nature of her existence and I was prompted to go into my world famous cowhide wallet in which I carried everything from Trojan prophylactics to Morse code procedures. I quickly whipped out a poem I had written and I thought it'd shed some light on the source of Marla's despair. It didn't, she hated the poem, but I also figured this would be a cute way to work it into this work. Here it is.

HELP!

I'm fat and ugly and stupid
Nobody loves me

And nobody worth anything will ever love me.

I have only one life

And already I'm molded.

I can't better myself.

I'm trapped in a horror show of loneliness ...

I'm tall and handsome and vibrant

My wife and kids and colleagues all love me.

But I'm stuck here.

I will never know true loneliness, pain, excitement or freedom

I've never really conquered anything myself ...

Richard V. Campagna

And soon I'll die. Having lived
with one one miserable frame
my whole life.

I'm doomed to be what I now
am. And this is how I'll be
remembered, if at all, Through-
out the depths of eternity.

HELP!

Marla went on with the same rap for about two hours and remarkably there wasn't one item in her virtual monologue that indicated insecurity or humbleness or exaggeration. Everything she said was totally true and I didn't even consider contradicting her. I told her I totally agreed with everything that she spouted forth and that out of affection I wished I could control my erections a bit better to get me to have sex with her. But I couldn't. She was grateful that I wanted to. By this time it was my turn to speak I didn't even want to. My problem was inconsequential. My quandary about Jeanette was the result of an absolutely absurd endeavor and I realized I had to be prepared to pay the fiddler if I wanted an opportunity to listen to his music. Jeanette was not going to read my mind and clearly, communicative contact would not be easy.

I hardly even broached the topic with Marla. I was really up for getting back to the apartment in Rhode Island and for laying the plans for my final attack. I further prepared myself for a tactical abandonment if my final attack was repelled. Being the heartless, unfeeling bastard that I am, I got my buckskin coat, at this point topped with soot and pizza stains and prepared to split. I left, Marla obviously realizing that I didn't need her any more and that was that. This world is really a cold place with guys like me walking around. I'm a selfish dirt bag and seemingly cannot love in the traditional sense of the word. All my love is, is a demand for security and a quick orgasm. I had a hamburger at Blimpie's and jetted (drove in a jet-like manner), up to Providence. Jeanette danced through my mind throughout the voyage.

Chapter XI

I hate the trip up to New England. It's long and dreary and full of smog and pollution and ugly cities, none of which I would live in. The food really, and I mean really, sucks ass in those Nutmeg Inns; the prices are total rapes and the gas goes for 45¢ a gallon for regular. I've made that round trip over twenty times and probably know the curves in the road better than I know those on the route to work.

I'm a bit down in spirit right now. My project is faltering to say the least and if I don't put something together pretty quickly I won't be able to keep your interest much longer. After all, you guys want something juicy to read, or at least something other than my inability to find harmony with mankind. Listen to some of my Fairchild college stories first and then we'll cut the diversions and get back to Jeanette.

Somewhat horny and lacking a substitute for Cindy, I consulted old reliable Jackie, my roommate engineer who suggested that I trek up to Fairchild College, a swanky four year college for bright (not brilliant) and extremely well-to-do young women. He said that although the girls were "succulent" looking, they could be extremely spoiled, materialistic and un-liberated brats, except for a select few. I figured that'd be okay for the time being, since at Bucknell I'd learned to deal with such types and I had a whole routine prepared for them. The only problem was to somehow get into the school and make an initial contact. Once that was accomplished I had enough confidence in myself to meet a shit-load of women, employing the snowballing technique. I was even willing to temporarily cover my pus pimple with a little bit of flesh colored Clearisil.

Jackie had a friend, Stanley Septimus, whose nickname was Septic Tank, a sophomore at Brown University. Jackie thought he'd be able to refer me to somebody. By the way, isn't it amazing that I never seem to think of anything other than women and yet I oftentimes exhibit disdain and disrespect for their feelings and emotions? Remember don't try to make sense out of me or you'll really get befuddled. Just flow with me, it'll be easier.

Anyhow, Septic Tank, a pushy Armenian from Long Island, with an answer for everything, had a whole list of people for me to meet. He was tall, had a bulging tummy, a big ass, a Bob Kauffmann Afro haircut, a dominant but not disgusting nose and a horrible Syosset accent.

"Listen man," he said. "I'll fix ya up with Lydia Penski, a dynamite chick from Port Washington. She's got nice tits, a tight ass, a good head and smokes a lot of dope."

I said that was O.K. but then requested something in the blonde division, straight out of Ashland, Ohio and fuckable as well. He said he had just the dish in mind; nineteen-year old Sandra Engstrom from San Rafael, California; blonde, blue eyes and tender thighs. That was all I needed to know and I left Septic Tank's room as soon as was humanly possible. His rolling machines, Pluto and

Goofy rolling papers, Playboy collection, little black book, poster of Castro eating out Pat Nixon and incense burning hippopotamus were causing my stomach to revolt.

I headed up to Fairchild immediately, weaving through the back-roads of the countryside towns of Attleboro and Horton. It's in Horton, Massachusetts that Fairchild is located, 19.6 miles from my house in Providence. Past Dunkin Donuts, Burger Chef, Jack's Roast Beef, Ho-Nam's Egg Rolls, Do-It-Now Car Wash and Horton Country Day School I sped. I stopped for an ice cream cone, coffee brandy to be specific and eventually found myself on Howard Avenue, an actual thoroughfare of the college.

Fairchild, founded in 1857 by some intellectual spinsters, is indubitably an exquisite campus. It's antique light posts give it the look of an early mid-western town, with rolling hills, a lake, a large indented piece of land affectionately known as the Dimple, a chapel, a store, a rickety old post office and a narrow, circular bicycle path. Sprinkled throughout the campus are old stone and wooden bridges which were unnecessarily constructed over the three babbling brooks that run through the college community. All of the buildings are either white, gray or beige and only three are modern in their architectural design. In the background one can see endless farmlands and miles and miles of country houses and places of business, running clear to Taunton. The college exudes antiquity, establishment, conservatism and tranquility. What the hell was I doing there?

It was a Wednesday night when I arrived. There were still some traces of snow scattered around. I headed over towards Elias Clark Hall, the dormitory of Sandra's residence and the newest building on campus. A big heavy set ogre woman in farmer jeans and suspenders looked out the spacious tinted window and continued to look me over as I entered the hall. She eyed me as if I were some greasy, dirty slime, ready to come in and take advantage of one of the girls. She was probably the house mother or something farcical like that, but I'll tell you that she could have found herself a lead part in a horror flick with very little effort.

I knew she'd think exactly what she did, so I figured I'd play with her a little. I pretended I didn't speak much English and from that she'd assume immediately that I was a Puerto Rican from Taunton or a Cape Verdean from Bristol who had no business at Fairchild. But before she could call one of the buffoonish campus policemen who roll tobacco faster than they can brandish their weapons, I told the old fart in my stylish radio voice that I had a date with Sandra in room 228. No problem getting upstairs.

I dug Sandra's appearance as soon as I saw her. Tall, thin, blonde, pretty and perfectly kept although she was not sexily attired. Already I could envision her in the rack.

She was well mannered, interesting to listen to, well read and coy, as are most girls whose fathers are in *Who's Who in American Business*. Her roommate, a Jewish woman from Miami was at her boyfriend's place at Brandeis, so the room was ours if Sandra got off on me. And she did, albeit only for one night.

I began to explain to her who I was and what I was doing in her room and then I commenced throwing my entire well-planned rap on her—that I was twenty-three, aware, cute, tough, rugged, well traveled, that I was a struggling young radio personality, that I had ambition, confidence, wit and that I'd visited fifteen foreign lands. We both popped two soppers on my suggestion, and in fifteen minutes we were both flying and horny as hell. In twenty minutes I had moved the two single beds together and in twenty-five we were undressed and humping wildly.

Her strong All-American thighs were wrapped around mine and she was throwing one of the meanest, tightest, classiest fucks I'd ever experienced. The girl was obviously horny and boy could she move. Her buttocks pulsated with emotion and mine obliged. My cock was as erect as it had ever been, at times almost throbbing audibly with power. The scum was dripping off my red tip, her cunt was wide, wet and beautiful. Actually the whole scene was beautiful in its own way and an aura of timelessness began to surround us. She blew me but it wasn't too good. She was not putting enough pressure on the head and something was lacking. I truly appreciated her genuine attempts. I came a total of four or five times and fell asleep totally exhausted. Before falling asleep we both heaped bilateral praise upon each other and before I knew it, it was 6:00 A.M. Thursday morning. I awoke with a monstrous hard-on. Sandra was fresh and marvelous looking under the sheets in spite of having popped a third sopper just five hours earlier.

After a good-morning fuck, I suggested we go to breakfast at the Student Union, vulgarly called the Cage. For some reason Sandra didn't want to go. She suggested a few places in town and became increasingly adamant in her stand not to go to the Cage. At first I took it for what it was worth and we agreed to go to Howard Johnson's in Pawtucket, one toke over the R.I. border. That was fine because I really groove on HoJo coffee anyhow. But in the car Sandra's peculiar silence made me stop and think for a while. Why was she against the Cage? Could it be that she didn't want to be seen with me? It seemed impossible based upon her bedroom performance but the thought did cross my mind and therefore was a possibility. I was in an honest mood and I asked her. She snapped back a no answer and her snappiness convinced me that her response was intended to be positive. She didn't want to be seen with a guy who was not an Adonis. It was as simple as that. While I was not unappealing sexually by any means, I was not a 6'2" jock, my look was far from All-American, my skin was far from commercial material and my hair was far from tidy.

I was fine in the bed for Sandra, but wasn't quite good enough for the princess to stroll into breakfast with to show off to her friends. Very helpful for the soul, isn't it?

I gave Sandra credit for her honesty and she proceeded to tell me of her parents' set of values making her prejudices readily traceable. Her mother was the head of the San Francisco chapter of the Daughters of the American Revolution and her father, the nephew of a former Secretary of Agriculture.

Sandra's not much different from most Fairchild women. They're pretty but rather unenlightened. The breakfast was a gas. I caught a twinkle in the eye of one of the waitresses and decided that some night I'd try get to know her. Sandra paid the bill and the tip and I took her back to Horton. I had gotten my rocks off but saw no potential for a future relationship per se. I busted the pimple again and let the pus drip on my chin and neck. "Fuck the Clearisil," I thought to myself. Already Jeanette had reentered my mind and I headed back to Providence to plan the next and perhaps the ultimate trip to Pacific Street.

Richard V. Campagna

Chapter XII

I'm back in my apartment now listening to the faint but undeniably phony laughter from Jackie's room. Jackie's here with his girlfriend who's quite foxy and very parochial and she protests marriage and the bourgeoisie so much that I believe that's where she really belongs.

I'm here with my pathetic excuse for sexual stimulation—my imagination and my five fingers. Like they say in *Hair*-masturbation can be fun.

Last night our landlady's niece came up from Newport and Renna, the yellow-teethed witch of a landlady with her sagging breasts introduced me to her. The girl, I believe her name was Malerie, had eaten two tabs of sunshine and was tripping like a mad woman when I first laid eyes on her. Renna, age 43, told her to come on up and visit the "celebrity" upstairs. Jackie always told me that I was the apple of Renna's eye.

Malerie was really cool. Her body was 100% porkable, a Bucknell expression for fuckable and her ass was so grabbable that I grabbed it within five minutes of our initial contact. She did protest not. Jackie, upon hearing that Malerie was tripping, figured that I'd like to join her in wonderland, which I did, whereupon Jackie, the king of

Providence and Bristol County mescaline dealers, laid two hits on me. I was off in a second.

Our trips achieved relative equality of intensity within one hour and Mal and I really got into some bizarre routines. We went out to the nearest McDonald's, got three or four shakes and proceeded to mush them in each others faces. We rolled around in bushes, mud, and even on tennis courts and eventually Malerie begun to hallucinate heavily. When she stopped, she started to blurt out something about going to the zoo, so we did, with Captain Feinstein at the wheel. No sooner had we arrived at Roger Williams Park when Malerie began to weep profoundly, inconsistently cackling something about herself being a baboon, who belonged behind bars. Acid, being easily five times as intense as mescaline, Mal's trip was like nitroglycerine compared to my chocolate milk one. I used whatever sanity I still possessed to alleviate her problems. I got her to the snack bar, bought some pop corn and sat her down under the nearest tree. Everything was fine; Mal had calmed down and I got her to massage my balls. I had called in sick to work the next day before I dropped the tab so there was no sweat about that. Wally "Chip" Hancock would do the news reports for me.

Work had been really shitty. I even gave some thought to quitting the glamor world of radio and going to law school or something—656 on the Law Boards, 706 on my GRE's. But I concluded that it'd be better to squeak out a few more paychecks until I could find a loan, a cheap graduate school or maybe even a more lucrative position. I thought to myself, "there must be some Jewish philanthropic organization which offers scholarships and if it came down to it I'd even brush up on my Hebrew." By the way I've given you no indication about the date or the weather, etc. It's February 23 and it's damn hot outside - maybe 55°.

Malerie and I were really getting off on each other's genitals and we wanted to ball on the spot. We were about to retreat 'neath a cluster of bushes behind the goose cage when suddenly, in a shrill release of tension and terror Malerie accused me of being a *"Scathing Jock"*.

I said to her, "What the fuck is a scathing jock?" and she began to babble out of control. I tried to comfort her but at the same time I still wanted to part the ruby red lips of her you know what, yet she would not let me near. My penis however, was very patient and due to the mellow nature of the organic mesc, I told it to calm down and wait a while. It obliged.

Malerie begged me to take her home and I did so without any further questions. There was no further communication between us as we reached our peaks and came down on some hash. She split to Aunt Renna's apartment and I to mine.

Later that same evening of the 23rd I went downstairs. Renna was at her Yoga lesson and Mal and I sat down to have some coffee and a bialy. Renna is half Jewish, Malerie's last name is Kaplan and we both like bialys. I asked her if she wanted to still fuck, did she still have any interest in getting to know me better and what the hell was a Scathing Jock? Her answers were somewhat unclear to put it mildly.

I left promptly after devouring all of Renna's lox and hit the sack. The next day I remained perplexed as to why Malerie didn't seem to dig me. In my most rational, existential and Laingian mode I dashed off a knot-like poem to her and left it on her dresser in the room where she was lodged. It read as follows:

> What I can't understand is why you treat me the way you do?
>
> By the way, the way you treat me is badly
>
> You don't appear to believe that I am an acceptable partner.
>
> There are only two real possibilities in the universe of your feelings; either you DO believe that I am an acceptable partner or you DON'T.
>
> These two choices encompass all possibilities of your inner feelings, regardless of your outward behavior.
>
> So, to analyze the way you feel, we look at the following:
>
> Either you dig me and you are pretending that you don't
>
> or
>
> You don't dig me and are acting exactly as you feel. If you dig me, why don't you act in such a contrary way? Do you think that I might not dig you?
>
> or
>
> Don't you know how to express your affection? If you think that I might not dig you, stop thinking that; I dig you. If you don't know how to express yourself, don't bother,—just say yes. If you don't dig me and are acting as you feel, why do you feel that way?
>
> Do you think I'm too ugly? or
>
> Do you think I act superior? or
>
> Do you think that I'm too stupid, too jocky?
>
> If you think I'm too ugly, then you're too stupid, too jocky.
>
> If you think I act too superior, just remember that I'm humbling myself now to gain your good graces.
>
> If you think that I'm too stupid, too jocky, then how could I

be so smart as to concoct this?

I guess I've gotten to all possibilities.

See you this Friday night at eight.

I got no response from Mal directly, and before I got to approach her on the topic of the poem she had left the city.

The next day I received a Special Delivery post card with a Newport postmark, with three boldly printed words—FUCK OFF JACKSON! I guess Mal didn't buy my "I'm O.K., you're O.K." mode of interrelating. I'd still like to know what a "Scathing Jock" is.

Chapter XIII

It's time for Jeanette plans once more. I know now that everything rests on my making positive, permanent contact. If I don't, my fragilely structured reality and sanity will take a severe blow, plus I won't get my rocks off and most unfortunately for you reader, my best selling masterpiece turns into an unmarketable truncated novelette.

I've picked the date of March 13 for my eventual conquest or ultimate figurative demise. I'm preparing like crazy for the event. Am on the grapefruit diet to smoothe out my sometimes flabby belly. I'm not eating any chocolate or pizza to clear out my system. I'm getting nice and relaxed, confident and cool. Even the job has been presenting fewer hassles and the people there are really getting off on my newly manifested mellow personality. The ditzy secretary, Joanne Martino, from Central High School, grabbed me twice yesterday morning. That was all I needed. I actually made out with her in the broom closet later that afternoon. Her tongue is really spunky, I don't mind admitting.

I was pondering whether or not to fly to New York but there were so many potential pitfalls I might stumble into, by being without wheels, that I figured it would be better to make the bullshit drive one last time. Between February 29 and today, March 3, I've been in what seems to be a different dimension. I can't remember what I've been doing, who I've been seeing or what I've been thinking. The only thing that's broken my trance has been a letter from my sister Andrea, a freshman at UW Madison.

Andrea and I are mutual admirers of each other. Ever since my parents separated eight years ago, we've grown ever closer. Andrea's looks have improved with the years. It's weird to see all your friends hitting on your little sister. She's gone from spunky looking to cute, to pretty, to adorable, to vibrant, to dynamite to gorgeous and her personality has developed correspondingly.

We're virtually the same in our feelings towards restrictions, structured boyfriends and girlfriends, hope, confusion and manipulation. We both understand what it's like to have some sort of manipulative control over others and we both quest to turn such dominance into honest, feeling love, while still maintaining respect. Seems like a mouthful but that's how we both feel. She is much more glamorous and middle class than I am. I, a little brighter, more honest and consequently more depraved than she. But together I know we'll work out individual life styles which emphasize freedom, truth, awareness and material well being. Andrea's letter, the last one I was ever to get from her, was remarkably short but dramatically cogent. It read as follows:

Dear Marty,

One thing I realized today is that college has made me feel how wonderful you really are. You have so much going for you and can get virtually anything you want. I wonder when I will figure out what it is that I need, but following your model I'll learn to take it slow and never commit myself until I'm sure.

You know what people want, think, need and feel based upon relatively little information. I see that ability slowly developing in me and at times it's a little scary to see all this power over others. Let's work together to use it for something positive.

I know you put me down for being so much into clothes and jewelry and sometimes I toss you off as being too "fuckin' weird", but let's never let things like that divide us. Each of us does these things as temporary escapes. See you Easter at Mom's house or maybe I'll drive up to Rhode Island. My driver's license becomes valid on the tenth day after my eighteenth birthday. Don't forget that date. I need a new tank top. I love you always.

Andrea

She's great. I love that girl more than anything. I'm like a different man when Andrea's magnetism is near and I know I'll continue to need her as she needs me. After receiving this letter, I could take on anything. Here I am Jeanette baby. This time I'm a comin' to you honey.

Chapter XIV

It's March 13, 8:00 P.M. I'm in a Brooklyn bar, drunk on my ass, but not delirious enough to forget about my writing. I had three shots of tequila, lemon, salt and the whole works and I'm flying. I'm drinking with two guys, one is blind and both are junkies. They asked me if I wanted some smack, just to try it. After we resolved the question in the negative, the guys laid off me with their rap and we talked a little more honestly. The place reeked from a mixture of sweat and alcohol. There were flies and ants galore.

My buddies' raps were simple. They needed money or dope and quickly. They had girls on the street and preferred prostitution to armed robbery and petty burglaries. One said that he had committed a robbery once, gotten away with seventy dollars, finally was apprehended, got off on a technicality and figured that it wasn't worth it. Think I was scared much? That's for sure. I think that this blind guy was also mute. If not, he had a pretty shitty personality.

The loquacious dude, who went by the name of Master Myke, must have been 6'3", lanky and bearded; more importantly he said that he knew Jeanette. In fact, he knew two Jeanettes but after careful analysis, I realized that he did in fact know my Jeanette Thompson, who he claimed was now 27, who was residing on Fulton Street and who did have a boyfriend-pimp and no children. Master Myke said that she was a "Fahne motha fucka, really fahne, perhaps too fahne for her own good." She never showed any emotions to her clients, nor to her cohorts, nor to the policemen who would occasionally bust her. She was a loner and loved to be alone. I bought Myke and myself one last tequila and as we downed them, the blind guy, Jesus (pronounced hey-SOOS) passed out on the floor. Time to see Jeanette.

Chapter XV

And sure enough there she was—just like I remem-bered her. She looked tantalizing from afar and I approached ever so slowly so as to be the only car around when I got to her. When I caught the first close-up glimpse of her face, a cold chill ran down my already alcoholically chilled body. Jeanette looked like a block of granite, cold, tough and not one bit compassionate nor understanding—not one bit.

I was too drunk to waste any time. In my usually chip-per voice I muttered. "Come on baby, I want a blow." She replied rather cautiously. "In the car that'll be $12." I said O.K. and immediately went into my rap. I couldn't lose even a moment this time and I was so loose that my words were dripping out of my mouth.

I began caressing Jeanette's legs, thighs and neck with my right hand as soon as she got in and she seemed responsive, whatever that would mean in this type of situ-ation. I went right for her mouth and kissed her with globs of saliva as I had done in my dreams.

She told me that the police were trying some new tricks to get the hookers off the streets, ranging from sincere let-ters urging reformation, to dressing up the lieutenants as grubby little johns. She said that she could tell that I wasn't a cop by my smile. Another propitious sign.

I pulled over on Nevins and Pacific and pulled down my jeans, put one leg on the seat and Jeanette really wanted to take care of business. Things were snowballing too fast. Thence far I'd accomplished nothing. Before she could start I blurted out something about my being a writer. Either she didn't believe me or didn't care because she approached my organ without a pause. Too late to revive the conversation. Her moistened lips surrounded my penis for the third glorious time, so soft, so round, so perfect. But before I even got hard, I came feebly and Jeanette very quickly opened the door, spit out my cum and lit up a Kool cigarrette.

"Boy," she said, "where you come from? If everyone came that fast, I'd be a millionaire. You don't have the clap do you? You can get hard, can't you?" And she sat there and continued to abuse me, calling me everything from a leper to a homosexual, or maybe it was the other way around. Finally, she demanded to get out immediately and she did.

I sat in my car totally dumbfounded still in a drunken stupor. I was a total fool to think that I could elicit any kind of communication for her. When I see how far away I actually was and how close I thought I was, it leads me to believe that my perceptive techniques are totally off base. She had no more interest in me as a person then she had in any inanimate object.

I guess she's just a whore I told myself. As I characterized her at the beginning, she's a capitalistically guided, street walking whore who doesn't give a shit about me or my existential framework or my droopy cock. But still, even if we are all whores in our own way, it seems to me that just maybe we can be whores to something real, something human. To be like Jeanette was to me is the most despicable way to treat a fellow human. I've been defeated in my immediate goal, but maybe I've learned something far more important. If I'm doomed to be a whore, let me at least whore myself to love, to sharing, to resolving the human tragedy and to hope. I drove back to Providence after three cups of Junior's coffee and three cheese Danishes. I did it in three hours and fifteen minutes—record time.

Chapter XVI

I had planned to give up this endeavor if I blew it with Jeanette. But I don't want you to leave me yet reader. You are probably the best friends I've got and I need someone to bear with me, especially at this time as I try to reconstruct my reality.

My sister Andrea, the love of my life, was killed last night in an automobile accident. Some punky rich kid in his red M.G. was trying to dazzle his passengers by dodging trucks on the expressway. My sister and her friend Maureen were in the car, all three were flung out when the car went berserk, the other two were not hurt and the car crushed my beautiful sister's skull to its untimely death. I hate that kid and his immature stupidity but the driver could have been me at age seventeen also. I am trying my best to transfer my hatred toward human impotency and mortality in general because if it remains funneled towards that kid, I'll kill him.

But Andrea's dead and I'll never see her again in this lifetime, perhaps never through the depths of eternity. I can just hope we'll link up again somewhere along the line so I can once again see her firm body, her white teeth, dark, soft skin and beautiful smile. I was her closest

Richard V. Campagna

companion and she was mine. Dead or alive I vow to make our duality stand.

My father, not my mother called me the night after I got back to Providence and in his most humane voice explained the horrible details of how we lost Andrea. I flew right back to La Guardia immediately and got there before the body arrived from Wisconsin. I had had it with Renna, Jackie and everything, and before I left, I told the radio station I was leaving for good. They were very kind and offered me two weeks extra paid vacation as I said with tears in my eyes that I'd be leaving and it'd be no vacation. I knew that my past was really my past and that I had to be off to New York to bid my sister good bye and then to God knows where!!??!!

I gave Jackie my shitty little stereo and grabbed my one remaining dark suit and two suitcases as I prepared for the bitterest two weeks of my life. I cried in front of all I met including the ticket seller, stewardesses and the cigar chomping taxi driver who zipped me from the airport to my mother's house.

I can't express to you the sadness I felt upon seeing my mom, my dad and my other sister and brother. We huddled together and cried, jointly, separately and then jointly again. The food, the flowers, phone calls, ruggelah and zeppole poured in as our souls poured out.

Andrea had a tremendous number of friends, many of whom appeared to be more aggrieved than we were. Together we pathetically tried to muster a philosophy of death, but each time we went flying on our faces. I, the reputed philosopher of the family was academic enough to check out what the masters had to say on the topic and I found that the Spaniard, Miguel de Unamuno helped the most although he also blew it on the last few steps.

I tried a thousand (ifs) to see whether there could be another situation worse than this. If I had died and Andrea had to suffer this way. If all three were dead and there were triple sufferings. That was useless. Then I tried some wishful replacement thinking. I wished my great aunt died instead or I wished that punky kid lost his miserable life. Certainly that did no good except to foster my vindictiveness.

I knew that rather than approaching this from a negative viewpoint I would try to preserve the beauty of Andrea's spirit so that I would never forget her tenderness, her concern, her hopes and dreams. To do this would be the closest I could come to making her immortal, and perhaps if these words get published, you readers will remember her also.

My mother is a Roman Catholic but we opted for a Jewish funeral. I asked the Rabbi if I might say a few words and he acquiesced. I could come between his enlogy and the prayers. But at the last minute he decided it would evoke too much weeping and personally I really didn't think I could deliver it without breaking up myself. In part it read as follows:

> At this time I am experiencing the most tragic and agonizing moments of my life. In this lifetime I have been robbed of the force that has helped me to destroy my cultivation of the absurd and to transform it into a love of the present and the future. With this in mind I hope I can transform the agonizing absurdity of this event into a remembrance of my beautiful sister that accounts for her true humanity and all of ours.

> Although we are each headed on the same course, the course of death, we all invent artificial goals for ourselves to give our lives meaning. But one of these invented goals seems less

absurd, less false and less contrived than all others. The goal that I speak of is consideration for others and helping them to avoid the absurd, helping them get through this lifetime. This was the goal of my sister, whether she truly realized it or not. She helped young people to face the paradoxes of their lives. She had a way of making them disappear in spite of the fact that they could not. This was the magic of Andrea.

Everyone here today was helped in some way by my sister. She never made sense of her own life, since she was too generous to do that. She got by, by giving others temporary answers, hoping that someday she could solve the enigmas of the universe for herself. She and I were a team, with this goal in our minds, and frankly speaking she kept the team together. Her patient ear and accepting eyes and sincere tears often took the place of her complete verbal comprehension of human weakness.

We on earth are the losers with Andrea's death. This is an undisputed truth. But let us hope that her soul, which I believe can never desist, has found contentment, peace and happiness. If we really feel for Andrea, and not only for ourselves, we must imagine her to be in bliss, as difficult as it may sometimes be. When I begin to waver I remember the powerful love manifested by her soul on earth and I know that this force is an indestructible entity. I know Andrea is at peace and I can feel it in the sky. That's all that matters to me.

The funeral was a beautiful tribute to her. The chapel was overflowing. People were hanging from the rafters to get one last glimpse of this princess's coffin. Then off to the cemetery and that's where I went to pieces.

Somehow when the casket is near you, you can feel the soul of the deceased surround you. To say good-bye to the casket is the saddest and truly the last good-bye. I cried for days, mostly to myself and decided that I needed to be with my family and friends. I lived at my mother's house and my father stayed there too. They might have even slept together for all I know.

Only the words of Abraham Lincoln kept me going.

"I too have suffered and know what I say well enough to tell you one thing—YOU WILL BE HAPPY AGAIN."

I learned how important it is to have friends. They help you get through crises of any magnitude, independent of any trivial bullshit. My parents' eight year separation emerged as the most trivial phenomenon of all, considering that when they really needed each other they hung together like an iron nail and an electro-magnet.

Our familial grief was so great that the draft board which was beginning to bug my ass at that point gave me a deferment for emotional hardship. I really needed it. And so did my parents.

What to do? No job, depleted savings account, no career, lost my sister and best friend and not even a real enemy on which to blame it, lost all sexual desires, philosophy of life was in shambles and I despised drugs. I did a lot of sleeping and a lot of weeping. Maybe it'd be a month before I'd be able to get myself together. But I knew it was time for a change—to gain the strength that I needed to live a life that could still be vibrant in spite of its tragic loss. Stick with me reader and I'll make you proud of me yet.

Richard V. Campagna

Chapter XVII

I stayed with my family in Brooklyn for a little over a month. My father moved back into the house that the courts granted my mother and they attempted to revive the angelic bliss that pervaded their marriage for the first 15 years. They actually did it, which showed that their disagreements were caused by pathetic inconsequential quibbling, at least from my vantage point.

And the family tried, incessantly tried, to rebound from our misfortune. Floss and Milt, my parents, were in the lead. Slowly but surely I too was casting off all the machinelike attitudes I'd acquired towards sex, women and humans in general. I was almost a human again, learning what it was to be alive, almost like a newly born child. I began to really get it together with my other sister who I'd neglected and probably even sub-consciously mistreated for her inability to be as perfect as Andrea.

I learned in one short month how to really respect people who were endowed with genes and chromosomes and mental processes totally different from mine. And with my younger brother, the eleven year old genius, I began to nurture and fortify our common levels of thinking. While Andrea had left us in the flesh, her spirit remains and serves as a kind of cement for our family bricks.

Life was great in Brooklyn without any responsibility, hassles or commitments. For thirty-six glorious days I was committed to living, to thinking and to being real. Miltie, my dad, a top notch tax lawyer laid $2,000 big ones on me, a rather generous offer. He said it was just because I was living that I received it and in effect he sounded just like me. I kissed my father for the first time since I was ten. Not because of the money but because for the first time he rewarded me for my realness and not for my alleged status or neurotic achievements.

What to do with it? One thousand dollars right into the Dime Savings Bank of Brooklyn. This way some interest could mount and I could get a badly needed hot comb as part of the bank's policy of benevolent bribery.

My days were constantly filled for the first two weeks of this mournful period. I read constantly—novels, existential psychological works, libertarian classics, women's literature, Chicano works of protest; you name it, I read it. I read in libraries, museums, coffee shops, at home, in the car and on my front steps. Pursuant to all this, one afternoon I made what might prove to be the most interesting discovery of my life: actually it was a re-discovery.

But before I get you inextricably involved in that, one other tid-bit of news. Some schmuck sideswiped me on my way home from Coney Island one night and sent me for a nice little stay in St. Matthews's Hospital of Brooklyn. So absurd was my accident and subsequent injury a mere two weeks after my sister's death that my condition produced more laughter than pity. While my stay in 306B was by no means super-exciting, there were some incidents of interest. I broke 7 ribs, had a 10% puncture in my right lung and my Buick was turned into a total accordion. Four other cars were smashed in all, two other people were injured—one broke his arm, the other a molar. The accident itself is a legal intricacy and the article about me in the Daily News was really a riot. Three girls from Great Neck called and said they'd seen my picture in the paper, thought I was cute and wanted to see if I was all right. They wouldn't leave their names or numbers though.

Chapter XVIII

My accident took place on the Belt Parkway, second only to the Long Island "Distressway" as far as inferior highways go. I was mauled by a hit and run GTO enemy driver. I swerved out of control, into the eastbound lane, and when you're on the wrong side of the Belt down around Sheepshead Bay, you don't really expect to escape without paying your dues.

Luckily I had the seat belt fastened and more importantly from a legal standpoint, there were no passengers in or around the death seat. All I can say though is that those broken ribs sure did hurt, and in fact still do. I thought I would expire at any time since I'd never experienced pain like that. I thought I'd punctured my diaphragm or my heart or my liver and really expected to die. It wasn't as sweet as I had anticipated in chapter VII. Thousands of people rushed to the scene, almost like a Bosco commercial-cops, construction workers, doctors, Jewish mothers and claim-hungry cigar chomping ambulance chasers. Within 15 or 20 minutes, a delightful St. Mattie's ambulance arrived. I never went unconscious which was one factor in my believing I was going to live on a little. But those little ribs really ached and pained upon every exhalation.

Richard V. Campagna

One doctor who arrived on the scene told me to sit tight in my Buick accordion and he turned off the motor but left the radio on. Some wacko disc jockey was giving a traffic report.

Finally the butchers in the ambulance arrived and if the on-the-scene doctor didn't tell them to give me some oxygen to alleviate the breathing pressure, I'd have broken in half. The ambulance driver kept telling me to "shut the fuck up" since he claimed it didn't really hurt and that I was a cry baby kid.

Got to the emergency room; the first problem was to tactfully inform my parents without catapulting them into a state of shock. The work horse of a nurse brutally arranged ten X rays for me and only one Jamaican X-ray technician treated me like a human being. The results, as I said, seven broken ribs, punctured lung (no collapse) and no hemorrhaging. Then a beautiful shot of pain killing Demerol and a call to my parents. They took it well, knew I was clearly going to live and that was that. The pain started to lessen, and with my life virtually intact I decided to make the best of the upcoming hospital vacation. Miss Scully, the emergency nurse jabbed my wrist with an I.V., just in case. It didn't even hurt.

Within twenty minutes I was wheeled into intensive care, but I really think I was just there for precautionary measures. They had the finest nurses there, attractive, dedicated, skilled in blood taking, shot giving and bedside conversation.

And they were good looking. Immediately they made me feel so totally at home that I knew I'd make the absolute best out of a normally shitty situation.

They wheeled me right next to the only other youngster

in I.C., a Peruvian girl, sixteen years old and really a beautiful person. Her hell-raising brother and she were also accident victims, but their outer shell was a V.W. bug and hence their injuries were much more serious than mine. The guy was out of intensive care, but the girl, Valeria, still had tubes in her lung, which did collapse. She was fighting off pneumonia.

Just as I put away my liquid diet lunch, consisting of juice, tea, soup, water, milk, jello and pudding, the team of Chinese and Indian doctors came in and mechanically yanked the three tubes from Valeria's side. She gave a sharp yell from the excruciating pain and in her cutest English accent, asked for a pain killer which she was immediately given.

Everyone else in the room had seen much better days and in fact one guy had just passed away from a heart attack. Most of the patients were over sixty, but the staff was so large that all of these needy souls got the best health care possible under the circumstances.

And I, not really about to give out a series of gifts causa mortis, got the advantages of constant bed watch, excitement, excellent food and nurses with the most interesting backgrounds.

I became very close to a really classy nurse, Chris Sheppard, tall, nicely built, beautiful blonde hair, tight and bright, and a delight to be in the same room with. She did about all one could do to dispel any ideas I had that nurses were competent sexual playthings for doctors. She was as smart as I am. She was trying to get a master's in Art History while she worked and she appeared to take a special liking to me and often sneaked me in extra meatloaf, cheesecake and O.J. It made it a pleasure to be cooped up. We talked about art, music and mostly medicine and I found her to be charming, ambitious and downright nice. And in spite of my drugged up relaxed body, sex was the furthest thing from my mind when I was with Chris. I'll bet you don't believe me, do you? I spent two days in Intensive Care on the same ridiculous basically liquid diet and got nicely addicted to those Demerol shots. When they told me for sure that there was no need to worry about a collapsed lung or latent pneumonia, I knew then that it was time to get ready to hang out in the storage area downstairs. Chris and another chick wheeled me downstairs to 306B and ironically enough, it was "sad" to be getting better.

My new room was kind of a dump. In fact, it was a veritable pit, but my new roommate was quite a blast. His name was Harry Yam, as in candied, his height 5'5", his birthplace Hong Kong. He was, and I surmise still is, a Professor of Communications at Columbia—sharp, funny, witty and moral, and in the hospital believe it or not, for a hypertension attack and for a circumcision. He'd just had his dick clipped when I arrived and a Haitian nurse's aide, Bonnite, was applying some ointment. He was wearing kubuki pajamas, and there were a few empty dishes and containers of bean sprouts scattered about the room.

We became friends instantly. The guy was fascinating inasmuch as he considered himself to be an Oriental Johnny Carson. He'd done a lot of MCing in Chinatown and actually had some proposals to do an English television program catering to the Chinese community of New York City. He spoke perfect Chinese, did some escort interpreting for the U.S. State Department, had a nice apartment on Riverside Drive and boy did his cock ache.

He was forty-two, looked twenty-three I'd swear, and had a very sincere, benign philosophy towards love, life and human honesty. He had a lot of girls come and visit him, mostly Chinese, all very graceful and super-intelligent.

He said he thought that I'd put it all together in five or six years and he called me a member of the new American intelligentsia. He indicated that he thought I would start a political movement meshing the political and the personal aspects of life. In every way he was very complimentary to me. He said I was quite an ass man, I guess because I too had a lot of female visitors. Old Harry and my parents also got along very well. They tossed around such topics as jobs, national security, Chinese and Italian cuisine and family life. Harry was really a panic.

Not much else went on during my recuperation period. All the nurses dug mine and Harry's asses since we were so comparatively young, funny, intelligent, cute and healthy. We weren't going to die on them.

Harry had talked me up to this one vivacious part time Candy Striper who fell immediately "in like" with me. She continually closed the curtains, changed my sheets constantly, grabbed my sweaty ass any time she could and finally started making out with me. She kissed O.K. and I don't really know why I got involved but I did, and for 4 days I had good morning, afternoon and before dinner French kisses from this sixteen year old medical volunteer. My diet had already been changed from liquid to solid. This girl claimed she had an interest in helping people, but also rapped endlessly about how she was a female ass-kicker for an Astoria Queens gang called the Tornadoes. Weird chick! They fired her on the fifth day of our budding relationship and that was that. Won't burden you by describing her any further.

Had a lot of visitors who were my parents' business and

social friends and while it was nice getting guests I would usually tire of them after two or three hours. One day an old friend of the family dropped my urine canister on Harry's chest and you can imagine the scene that resulted.

Did some Spanish homework for some of the nurses and even wrote a paper for an NYU English major nurse on Joseph Conrad's THE SECRET SHARER. This girl, Pat, another nurse, was twenty-five and from Jamaica, West Indies. She was super quick and very sarcastic. Two days before I was to leave I decided to dash her off one of my inimitable letters. She answered with a card and a poem but I could tell she didn't want to see me again in any serious form. I think she was married to a Jamaican rock-singer. In any event, in my letter to her I was able to organize my thoughts on life and death in the aftermath of the accident and to include such now might be helpful in figuring out the direction in which my whirlwind life was heading.

Dear Pat,

First of all let me say thanks for your flattering words and expressions throughout my hospital stay. I truly believe that with your sincerity and a little luck and a hot shit agent, you'd probably make it on the stage as a serious dramatic actress. However with your "secure Jamaican womanhood" I'll bet you'd like to think and communicate and feel for yourself, and those you love and have no desire to become a commercial product.

Secondly let me tell you that as I sat in this bed last nite, alone, I started pondering themes of immortality and you seemed to come to mind for reasons that I'd like to explain below:

Every time I meet someone in this world I'm plagued

with the choice of continuing a relationship in some form with this person or of resigning myself to the finite fact that our first crossing of spirits may be the last throughout eternity.

It sounds like a pretty fucked up melodramatic way of phrasing the desire or lack of desire to keep up a friendship, but to me such a choice has taken on far reaching philosophical implications.

My original philosophy of this topic was more or less as follows:

ALL HUMANS QUEST TO BE IMMORTAL, TO LIVE FOREVER TO ACCOMPLISH EVERYTHING TO BE LIKE GOD-BUT THEY KNOW THEY ARE DOOMED TO FAIL-THEY ARE IMPOTENT BLOBS, FINITE IN NATURE AND SLAVES TO THEIR OWN PARTICULAR BODIES, TALENTS AND BACK-GROUNDS.

YET IN SPITE OF THIS WE CAN CONTINUE OUR QUEST FOR IMMORTALITY. ACT AS THOUGH WE COULD DO EVERYTHING AND DEVELOP A QUIXOTIC FAITH IN OURSELVES-FAITH THAT OUR SOULS ARE INDESTRUCTIBLE AND OUR MINDS INFINITE.

Such a philosophy I believe to be very brave, courageous and optimistic, but unfortunately in practice it became unworkable. As my mind strove to be immortal, my body and emotions tried to follow suit. They couldn't keep up tho. I tried to get my grubby little paws into every door-teaching, entertainment, writing, athletics, traveling, broadcasting. I could go on for days. And such a quest extended into my social life. I tried to become friends with every one I met and lovers with just as many. Every moment became one in which to make a crucial choice and for me, to let something slip out of my grasp was to lose it for all eternity-be it a person, a thing, a quick fuck or an experience.

This little accident and another automobile accident which caused the death of my beloved sister, really whipped the aforementioned philosophy into a different form. Without wedging my personality into a nook, let me say that my rap now reads something like this:

AS HUMANS, WE ALL QUEST TO LIVE ON FOREVER. WE ALSO QUEST TO JUMP OUT OF OUR BODILY SHELLS, OUR MENTAL LIMITATIONS AND OUR ECONOMIC ENCUMBRANCES. BUT WE CAN'T. THE BEST WE CAN DO PRAGMATICALLY IS TO GET THE MOST FROM OUR MINDS AND BODIES WITHOUT TURNING INTO NEUROTIC ACHIEVERS AND WITHOUT FORESAKING FUN, LOVE, FREEDOM AND JOY. WE MUST SEARCH FOR A BROADNESS, FIND OUR LIMITS, STRETCH THEM TO THEIR FULLEST POTENTIAL AND THEN STOP. BUT OUR MINDS HAVE NO LIMITS. WE CAN IMAGINE ANYTHING. IT IS THERE THAT WE CAN BE EVERYTHING. IT IS THERE THAT WE CAN CULTIVATE A FAITH IN IMMORTALITY; WE DON'T NEED ADVENTISM, JUDAISM, MARXISM—WE JUST NEED OURSELVES.

My aching ribs now show me my true limits. My dead sister shows me that what's really important in a human being is his or her soul, which always lives as far as I'm concerned. There's no need to dwell on these ideas with others. They're personal and now I can go about my life, free from nervous quests to conquer and ready to be both broad and mellow in tandom.

As to interpersonal relations let me add that the old Marty would have taken the names and addresses of 10 or

15 girls that he met in the hospital. But the more mature Marty knows that you can't have ten new relationships that would turn out to be worthwhile. The new Marty realizes his outer limits and tries to pick and choose, the competing factors being self-gratification and at the same time potential benefits to the outside world. And when the new Marty feels limited he now turns inside to grow and experience.

I hope that sometime we'll be able to get together. I know you love your boyfriend or husband, whatever he is, and that he loves you and I know you're smart enough to know that I'm not throwing any bullshit moves, couched in my philosophical framework.

I'd just like to do something with you sometime. Go to Coney Island, see a play, get drunk, see a basketball game, go to a museum or just sit and listen to music. The choice is yours tho...

I hope you're as happy, as funny, as alive, and as confident as ever and I hope your boyfriend is treating you as you deserve. Furthermore I hope this letter didn't offend you in any way. You had a big effect on me and I wanted you to know it. If you ever need any help, just let me know.

Love

MARTY

Pat delayed a while and eventually I got this poem in the mail in response-

THANK YOU!

You are beautiful—
Not because you expressed your ideas on paper.

Not because your intellect is advanced, but because you are simple.

You are simple—
because you are unaffected
because you share your knowledge
because you can relate on all levels.

Words seem hard to describe your personality.
I can only rejoice
I encountered you in Salvation History.
Take care of yourself–Many, many thanks and keep up the good
work.

Patricia

I also left one last poem with my Haitian friend, Bonnite, an expressive and friendly comical work, if I do say so myself.

BONNITE

I have met an extremely fair lady
From the tropical island of Haiti,

Her back rubs and chills,
Take the place of my pills,
A reminder of "succulent Katy."

But Bonnite is by far number one,
For her touch all the Haitians do run,
Even young Pappa Doc

Sets his time by her clock,
And waits for her voice in the sun.

She has grace like a Roy Rogers stallion,
Her eyes glow like a taxi medallion,
She calms down the vultures,
By her mixture of cultures,
Her first husband being Italian.

Her skin and her touch are so fine,
Like I said her black eyes sure can shine,
If she hangs me tonite,
I will soon catch a fright,
If she comes I will sleep so divine.

Oh Bonnite, please come, make me feel better,
Take my praise through this passionate letter,
My backside is aching,
My ribs they are breaking,
My skin's like a tight clinging sweater.

Richard V. Campagna

Chapter XIX

So much for the hospital. I spent a handful more of uneventful days there and knew that I had to begin to think of what to do for the summer. The ribs were getting better, I was off my narcotic and had no job. What the hell to do?

My next to last day in the hospital I made this rediscovery that I alluded to before. I rediscovered Brazil after a three year respite. During my junior year at Bucknell I took a course in introductory Portuguese. My Portuguese mentor, Dr. Alberto Vieira, a carioca (native of Rio) and also a fanatic Brazilian had painted a very dynamic picture of his vast homeland throughout the course, and his ability as a professor and as a person influenced greatly my developing fluency in the language by the end of my senior year. In fact I had even considered going to graduate school in Latin American Studies but the radio job in Providence popped up and I lost whatever contact I had with Portuguese, Emerson Fittipaldi, Pelé and the entire Luso-Brazilian world.

But the hospital library for some reason unbeknownst to me had some Portuguese books in stock and after reading the Brazilian journalistic classic, OS SERTÕES, by

Euclydes da Cunha, my Portuguese began to flow again and my interest in Brazil regained some of its momentum. My Latin blood began to boil with thoughts of samba and soccer and sun and women and rum and Brazilian cuisine.

My first day out I headed to the Brooklyn Public Library's Midwood branch and by the third day the librarian thought that I was Portuguese for sure. Every day she'd have new books, journals and essays waiting on her desk for me. She gave me info on Brazilian radicalism, the role of the Brazilian military, the tragedy of the oft-neglected northeast, tort law in Brazil, the subtle racism of the Brazilians, the developing Amazon basin, the rich cattle ranches in Rio Grande do Sul, the mystique and dependency of Brazilian women, the psychology of soccer (futbol) and the role of carnaval in the Brazilian personality.

I had three Portuguese grammar books (one written by Vieira himself), and three huge dictionaries, a book of 201 Portuguese verbs, pronunciation flash cards and the whole works. Every date I had would culminate in a Brazilian restaurant on 46th Street in New York City, so I could cultivate even further my accent (sotaque).

And logically enough my mind soon resolved to actually head off to Rio. I'd take my $1,500 and new hot comb, three pairs of corduroys, my recently revitalized knowledge of Brazil and its customs, plus my English speaking ability and see if I could make a go of it in Rio. What did I have to lose? Nothing, and a whole new start and life style to gain. And if there were no future for me there, I'd at least get a great vacation.

I found a study group, the Brazilian Summer Study Group, a Rio organization which offered graduate courses in Botafogo for one month and a second month which was a free show. The cost for the 62 days would be $675, certainly a fair deal, so I immediately signed up with Mark Sanders, the program's founder, capital supplier, director, professor, publicity agent and general hot shit ombudsman. The group of 160 from all over the U.S. and Canada was slated to leave on June 13. The time really flew by, and I was thrilled about a new set of circumstances, I still longed for Andrea but derived newer and realer ways to perpetuate her memory. Everything was great.

Chapter XX

But trouble soon struck as it always does when things go well in this roller coaster world. My oldest and dearest male friend, Henry Schweitzer, who goes by the nicknames of Big Poppa Jerome, Big Poppa, Big Daddy, Dungeon Breath, Maniac Man, Schizoid Man, Shemper and Dragon Head, now hates my guts. The provocation was slight but so was the assassination of the Serbian duke. A little background information is in order.

Henry and I had grown up together and many said he followed my every move. He'd contradict himself unmercifully just to be on my wave-length. Our mutual friends constantly accused him of having no mind of his own, of being my lackey, my answer man and of getting into everything I did, but only one week or month or year later. Henry even applied to Bucknell and didn't get in. While on the surface it might appear as if he were a carbon copy of me, I always liked to think that it was merely a question of our both having the same interests, goals, fears and perceptions, with me being perhaps a little better at organizing, articulating and projecting. I also think I had a little more confidence and a lot more guts.

The congruency of our ideas became even more

apparent when we both went through a period of "anguish." The period which we went through jointly, consisted of total depression, lack of relevance, sharp flashes of schizophrenia, fear, sexuality disappearance and at times hallucinogenic paranoia. I, being the so-called academician tried to intellectualize the whole thing and luckily I did, as I coined the term "existential anguish" to describe our feelings. Together we put together such a cohesive but gloomy "rap" that a mutual friend of ours, Matzoh Ball Goetz, a court stenographer, said that he'd heard each of us give the speech and there was at most, a deviation of ten or fifteen words throughout the entire presentation.

We came out of the anguish at different times and each of us was getting into different things for the first time. He never put me down for any of the stupid things that I was into, but unfortunately I, the snob, would make fun of his hippie games—he got into revolution, making water pipes, bongs, photography and of all things, plumbing. He was very close to Andrea and would make it with her once in a while and probably loved her almost as much as I did.

He had just graduated from Hobart College in Geneva when Andrea died and was continuing to live in Geneva since he'd signed a one year lease and had no place better to go. Henry was a good poet, but for a while he began to think he had a financial future in it. He had also expressed an interest in becoming a plumber since he had become totally disheartened with the academic community.

During my stay in Brooklyn, I dashed him off the following note. It sure turned out to be the straw that broke the camel's back and it set off a mighty interpersonal explosion.

The correspondence went as follows and to this day I don't know who's in the right. A clear case of unreliable narration. Let the reader decide: So reader, go ahead and decide. In any event, Henry and I don't speak much any longer, and it seems that warring factions have banded around us, embracing each one of our particular life styles. Mind you, we were best friends and should have been able to say whatever was on our minds to each other. The letters read as follows:

(1) Dear Henry,

You're out of school. Let's face it. If you want the bread you've always said you did, you'll need a profession—it's either law or medicine or teaching. You say you want to be a poet. Not desirous of casting any aspersions on your work, let me just say that poetry is a field that demands greatness not just mediocrity. And if you go into plumbing I doubt your poetry will have much credence in the academic community.

Also, you say you get off on Sandi (a mutual 17 year old friend of ours.) I think you're kidding yourself. To act as if she can understand your life is to dupe yourself on a groundless desire. The chick is a twirp.

Love, Your best friend

Marty

(2) Marty,

What you say about Sandi is your own opinion; your own thoughts and feelings. Why do you still keep any kind of relations with her? I don't know why you keep telling me about Sandi and her faults. I have many of my own—but to be hypocritical is to be deceiving yourself. What I am astonished at tho, is your feelings and thoughts about me.

You see—I have gone through a lot of thinking and self-discovery on my own for a long time now. I've always realized that you are paranoid about many things and in different ways. But to put me down for being creative is too blatant—even for you. To tell me where I stand as an individual is too fucked up even for you to expect me to believe.

I won't argue with you or be defensive by telling you that I am good at writing or that I am a good plumber or whatever. I will say that you've become a hard, cruel, unfeeling person in many ways and very non-adept at not exposing it. You see, I don't really expect you to be happy that I'm happy. I know that's not how you work. But, at any level, to try and tell me that I as an individual have fewer alternatives at being happy than I as an individual think I have—well fuck off buddy cause I don't dig that. Don't try to make me unhappy again Marty. I mean your letter was too low for me to handle.

I'm getting angry now, I'll have to calm down. You've got to realize a lot more about yourself before you make any more intense realizations about my future. I'm not ready to limit myself.

Your letter made me unhappy—something I never tried to do to you. I never try to bum out a good friend. It's against my nature. But now I realize that some type of confrontation is at hand.

My creativity makes me happy. Your creativity is in manipulation. Manipulating people—You've done it with Ronan for a long time. Behind each of our backs you've manipulated us. But I never cared to confront you because you're my good friend. I don't like to make waves. I never got into any arguments with you because I don't like that. But now man, you have upset the balance. Even during the summer you put down our "Musketeer's Club" for getting high and then you would drop a sopper and ball Susan. Man you're really getting fucking blatant these days. Why do you have to bum me, your best friend out?

Do I have to be a mirror image of you to be a person? What's the matter? Maybe you ought to see a shrink. I don't know Marty. I don't want to be made unhappy by you—you're gonna have to find out who I am. I guess it's partly my fault for letting you order for me in restaurants all the time. But what you're doing and what you've done has hurt many people and now you're hurting me. But I'm immune now mother fucker—but I'm also concerned about you—Just like I've always been. Don't pull your political games on me Marty. I won't listen.

I mean you're telling me if I want to live it's either a profession or else nothing. You're dead wrong. Living is a total experience, as existentialism says it is. You're no existentialist—neither am I. I don't want to be. You pretend to be one. Man you've got a lot of value arranging ahead.

One day maybe we'll bring everything out in the open—if you are up for it.

You're always categorizing and putting things in certain analytical niches when there is really no need for it. I realize that is the way you think and it's fine with me—it's always been O.K. but now you're imposing—something I just won't stand for.

I guess you've always imposed. But now it's too one sided to ignore. In the past when you spoke to me about our friends Sandi and especially Ronan I always felt strained. There was no need to win me over or whatever you were doing. I happen to like and enjoy Ronan. He is one of my best friends. I never knew why you held something against him. You really can't stand seeing someone expanding or enjoying themselves—can you? Just stop subjecting me and others to your scrutiny like you have been. You've pushed Ronan away, and now you've done it with me. You would have succeeded a long time ago but I threw it off as being your way of relating to people.

You don't like people who disagree with you. You are envious of others' worthy characteristics.

I hate writing this letter—but I won't be fucked with again. You've hurt me and you have done people wrong. People who like you for being you—not for your rap, not for existential big talking and not for manipulating.

I don't know If anyone along your line has even approached you in this manner before, but independent of that I certainly have that privilege. I don't want to come off sounding like God or the Spanish Inquisitor. Just a friend who's looking out for his friend like he always has. Accept me for me-not for someone you want me to be—

Love, Henry, Big Poppa,

Jeremy and anything else.

PS. I am your friend—to ignore your last letter and further confrontation would disqualify me as any sort of a friend of yours—I never dig upsetting the balance—But I had to.

My immediate response:

(3) Dear Big Poppa,

I am growing a little weary of trying to figure out which of us has the problem. If I am so paranoid about my life style and fascistically have to force my patterns upon you then I truly do have the problem. If you are so paranoid about not having a career and financial independence and have to justify your choice by accusing others of trying to limit you, then you truly have the problem.

But joint problems, singular problems or no problems, that's the way it goes and it seems like we're both getting by and that's enough. I'm content to leave things the way they are and take things for what they're worth.

Hopefully I can at least write this without the fear of igniting another vindictive rage on your part. Let's do this. Let's leave things in the worst interpretation for both of us. I'm an encroaching, hypocritical fascist snob and you're an unsure little kid, desperately trying to justify your unproven ways. If we accept this much, then nothing can get worse—only better.

You must admit it's kind of fun having a friend that you despise.

Marty

Anyhow the fight ended with nothing more said. In retrospect, it looks like I was more in the wrong than Henry was. In any event all of my Brooklyn friends and I spent my remaining time in New York together. Henry, Ronan, Cheese Whiz and I were inseparable prior to my departure for Brazil and the night of my flight we all got high and trucked out to La Guardia Airport. It was the beginning of some exciting new adventures. I still missed Andrea, as always.

Richard V. Campagna

Chapter XXI

The night was June 13. The weather, clear and breezy. We were all in Cheese Whiz's Rambler Rogue, 1960 model, steaming down the Interboro Death Trap to give me a rousing send-off to South America. The others were high on hash and soppers. I was relatively straight. Cheese Whiz, the real maniac of the foursome was driving the car with his nose. He'd learned to do that in Argentina, his birth place, where apparently the people really get off on balancing things on their noses. Anyhow we got to La Guardia at about 8 P.M. and the plane was slated to split at 8:30. I bought the guys a drink. Henry had to get to sleep early and so they left me. I was alone and alive. I was going to be on Sugar Loaf within 15 hours.

Once by myself, I started looking for some ass immediately. Incredibly enough, within 5 minutes I had exchanged glances, words and a quick touch with the girl who was to prove to be the best blow job west of the Rockies and as far as I'm concerned, east of them as well. Well she's tied with Jeanette anyhow.

The name, Roseanne Block. Five feet six inches, blonde, her rap: Brazilian studies and free sex, her part-time job a masseuse in Berkeley. She was with some

California creep who thought I was an East Coast ethnic creep as well, but luckily enough, Roseanne seemed more interested in the ethnic looking New Yawka than in him. We all boarded the Varig jet in great spirits and we all sat fairly near to each other. The takeoff was pretty decent.

Chapter XXII

So that's what I've been into all year. And now you know me and we're virtually up to date and we can travel jointly. That's why I like to write so much. You can actually make friends through paper and ink in very short time periods. In case you've forgotten, we're back on the plane.

I had a good sleep while you people read about my past and then I awoke, but most importantly, upon wiping the crust from my eyelids I realized that Roseanne had left the Disneyland creep during the course of my snooze and was next to me in Seat 10E, with her dacron coat on 1OF to avoid any unnecessary intrusions.

We watched a Bob Hope movie together. Bob balled some Indian squaw near Wounded Knee, South Dakota and a war ensued between the honorable Sioux and the U.S. Army. Bob tried to play an inept mediator, still grabbing tons of sex throughout and eventually had to flee into the Black Hills for his life.

Roseanne was not a beautiful chick, but her straight blonde hair, and super tight ass certainly caught my interest. We conversed well in English, Spanish, Portuguese and even a little French and after my third rye and ginger and her third Miller she put her head on my shoulder, we fell asleep and we played with each other throughout the night. I came twice and Roseanne was pretty hot herself but the frustration eventually manifested itself about three or four in the morning. My hard-on would reach a certain threshold and then virtually collapse in disgust. Blue balls they used to call it. Roseanne really could kiss and whether she learned her techniques from Beach Boy movies or from actual practice, I could have cared less at that point.

When we awoke we both felt fairly decent as opposed to the normal raunch that usually sets in after 8 hours in flight. We both totally slept through our touchdown in Caracas, but who gave a shit. Within one hour after beholding the early morning raging sun, we were to touch down at Galeão Airport on the outer limits of Rio.

The entire descent and landing were overwhelming and thunderous applause let the captain know that his work didn't go unnoticed. My joy upon stepping foot upon Brazilian soil could be seen by the tenseness in my facial muscles. I just wanted to bellow. But there was no time. There was a mad rush to get to and then through customs first and I was swept along with the crowd.

Chapter XXIII

Roseanne and I split up since our baggage was deposited by the baggage wheel at different times but we agreed to get together before long. The program director, Mark Sanders was right at the gate with a sloppily printed sign which had words to the effect that the group should get itself together in a huddle-like mass, near the coffee stand. The outdated, understaffed, un-air conditioned airport was a total madhouse.

The first male member of the group that I had the pleasure to meet was Howie who was later to become known as the Magrinho, Portuguese for the little skinny fart. He was short, maybe 5'4", thin, sickly looking, grubbily bearded and had the creepiest voice you'd ever care to hear. His lips repulsed me the most for some reason, since they were so thin and shapeless and red and pimply and chapped and everything else that could possibly be wrong with lips. I can still hear his stinging voice saying dumbass things like "000h, Coodie, and Copacab (anne) ah."

He had taken his previous summer vacation in Saigon which shows you how nuts he really was, although I must admit that the stories he had to relate about the tragedies of war and suffering and hunger and disease were both accurate and heart rending, even to me. He rapped a lot about his mother and in addition, demonstrated intense paranoia in regard to things like being enclosed, getting mugged, getting rejected and being accused of being a faggot (homosexual). He was sporting two different colored socks, his shirt had ketchup on it and he had no belt. One belt loop was missing. He had a ring in his left ear. He was to be my roommate.

When I shook his hand I could have pulled it off. It was like shaking hands with a salami, or even worse, a shrimp salad sandwich. I could tell that I alienated the dude immediately and I could tell he thought that I thought that I was too cool for my britches. He didn't like me; that was apparent.

Most of the crew got their bags and Sanders, the slender, sophisticated Minnesota born mentor of this incredible package deal, arranged us in foursomes in Brazilian made taxis and shipped us to our delightful abode, the HOTEL TURISTICO. The fare was 20 cruzeiros per person ($3.25) plus 5 cruzeiros for a tip. A cruzeiro was worth about 16 cents at the time.

The Turistico, now almost a legend for Americans in Rio, is located on the twisting, cobblestone hill called the Ladeira da Gloria, just minutes from luxurious Flamengo Beach. Next to the Hotel is the historical Igreja da Gloria, a 17th Century church where miracles are said to occur fairly often. The church is open twenty-four hours a day and when tourist and workman alike feel needy or guilty or happy or worthy, there's the good Senhora da Gloria to soothe their woes or uplift their spirits.

As we arrived (about 50 of us were lodged at the Turistico) the excitement began to mount, both for us tourists and for the money hungry tour mongers who wanted some of our rich, green dollar bills. We got a quick sour taste of Rio on the ride from the airport to the hotel and got to smell the pollution, the rancid wine and rotten meat aromas; we got to take in a slew of beggars, the raunchy coffee stands, the hustling people and the maniacal bus drivers. When we got to the hotel, the Brazilian and Chilean help were ecstatic upon learning that we were Americans and they could already smell the fresh, crisp dollars and feel the big, juicy boobs on the American girls, all of which they expected to be total sluts. Naturally; they were from the U.S. of A. Boy, were they ever wrong on both counts!

It seemed that of the fifty-two of us who ranged in age from eighteen to sixty-two, myself and a Portuguese grad student from Oregon, Ellis Harper emerged as the leaders. We two spoke the best Portuguese, she had the vocab and the culture down pat and I had the accent; together we turned out some dynamic Portuguese expressions. We arranged all the collective bullshit and it took us almost four hours to get all the others into their respective rooms. We haggled over towels, curfews, women/men coming into the rooms, price of rooms and payment plans but we mistakenly forgot to search for any homosexuality issues among roommates. I suffered for that lapse. Howie was gay (to be discussed later). First and foremost, let me paint the picture. (See following page).

Such was our team of "gringos" in the hotel. Cipriano was the owner but he worked his ass off behind that desk anyhow, afraid his help would rob him blind. His two nephews, Elifas and Waldo, often seen flanking him, have been working there since they dropped out of the Brazilian equivalent of grade school some 6 years ago. Edite, translated as Edith, was the maid and all purpose, "hotel mother". She had marital problems, very few teeth (those she did possess were quite yellow from placque) and she suffered from a horrible limp. Forget about the nasty scar on her forehead. She was incredibly kind and if you didn't get too close and come face to face with her dragon breath, you could definitely get to like her. Before she even found out my name she begged me for flowers and/or perfume and being the old softie that I am, I gave her my word she'd have them in great quantities before I departed the country.

The only other member of the staff was Francisco, the deaf/mute cook from Barcelona. He was a nice guy but not much on interpersonal relations. He served us the same goddamn breakfast for thirty-two straight days before he finally backed down and served us Gouda cheese instead of Brazilian white cheese. He soon switched right back. Of the two nephews, Elifas was horny but Waldo was even hornier. Cipriano was a prude, but we expect it of him since he was born in the Galician highlands, in a province near the Portuguese border with Spain.

The hotel could have been standing during the days of the peaceful revolution of Brazil in 1822. There were balconies and flower gardens, and stucco walls and all sorts of old-fashioned dumb-waiters. That's how quaint this place was. The keys to the doors were skeleton keys and the doors to the kitchen and the little bar (barzinho) were like the 1890 saloon doors pictured in Bat Masterson flicks. All of the help looked as if they'd seen better days, but they kept awake by pumping little Brazilian coffees down their gullets, known popularly as cafezinhos. They consistently got the job done for us all.

What can I actually say about the hotel. The 52 of us were there trying to squeeze some excitement out of something that ostensibly had none. Not the city mind you—just this quaint little hotel had none, at least to begin with. But we found some and generated more and more and by the time we started classes, the adjoining bar had become a well-known night spot in Rio's Gloria-Flamengo section. A crummy little joint mushroomed into a hedonistic sophisticated pleasure spot.

We all got used to our quarters. And after all the bull-shit was over for the day we all went upstairs to the one-bedded, one-windowed, one-dressered rooms and slept for a good 15 hours in the delightful night time air of the mild Brazilian winter.

HOTEL TURISTICO

Ellis Annette Sydney Ursula	4 Nebbishes	Jack Victor Steve Claude	4 Forest Rangers on Geological Research	4
2 married couples sharing suite	4 ?	4 ?	4 ?	3
Howie and yours truly	Gregg and Mark	4 Nebbishes	4 more	2

Goldie	Bagman Bernie	Candido	Bill	Old Sara "A Velha"	Chick from Wash.	Lisa	1

Cipriano Elifas Waldo

Main Desk

Edite
Maid

Lounge Francisco
(cook)

Chapter XXIV

Sanders, the dapper dude, got us all together the next morning for a one hour orientation. Of the 50 tid-bits he mentioned, only three would have any bearing on our well being while in Rio. But the guy obviously had personality problems and liked to hear himself talk both in English and Portuguese, so it became jokingly fun for us to listen to him ramble.

He told us that if we wanted to give someone the finger in

South America we should do this

instead of this

because this had no significance in Brazil.

Secondly he told us how to make a phone call with a little token called a "ficha" and thirdly he told us not to confuse the word "ficha" with "bicha" cause bicha means "homosexual" in Portuguese. Everything else Sanders blurted out was a complete waste. Luckily for his ego however, the elderly Jewish couples from Queens and Philadelphia were impressed by his bi-linguality so that at least his masters' from Georgetown didn't go to waste totally.

After his speech we all got up and started to attack the city like little vermin. Seriously now, Sanders did tell us some things of import, the full import of which didn't manifest themselves to me until I really needed them. To this day I thank Sanders for his explanations. Immediately after his discourse I decided to bag the study part of his operation entirely. I awaited the chicks, the beaches, the Brazilian mountains, the sharp, quick Latin life style and the sun. I vowed that I'd be as happy as I could in Rio, that I'd examine (and experience) as many women as I could, and that I'd swim up a storm.

Chapter XXV

Sara N. Meltzer, age 62, weight 132

My first real night in Rio I spent with a 62-year-old nymphomaniac. She had been eyeing me on the plane and I paid her no attention but in the lobby of the hotel we had a very nice conversation and I took her out for a beer (cerveja) during the afternoon. I told her to have a good day and erased her from my slate.

When I came into the hotel about 9:30 that evening to change my dungarees, she was there alone, leaning against a banister outside my room and was obviously drunk. I asked her if I could help her and she immediately threw her arms and body around me. Then as I was about to ask her a question she planted a huge, walloping kiss on my lips with her bright orange lipstick. Actually it wasn't a bad kiss.

I was drunk myself and although I was nowhere as drunk as she was, I decided to kiss her back. We did this a few times and then it occurred to me that I was probably kissing someone as old as my mother—maybe forty-six or so. I decided to stop then and I asked her where her room was so I could help her get to bed and then take off. She suggested that just for the fun of it we go to bed and I don't know what kind of bug I got in my head, but the combination of horniness, desire to try everything in this lifetime, drunkenness and the South American air made me take her up on it. At least I was willing to try her out.

I immediately pushed her into my room before anyone could see and since I knew that Howie would be out for a couple of hours more, there was no need to fear any embarrassing interruptions. No one saw us go in.

"I really think this'll be fun," she cackled.

"What makes you think that?" I returned.

"Oh, I don't know. But when I was Miss Atlanta in 1933 all the guys said I was the best lay east of the Rockies."

"Well Sara, I said, "Let's hope they were right. Please take off your clothes."

She stripped so rapidly that I didn't even see how she got her smock off but to be honest with you I sure wish she'd left it on. Her body was a total disaster area. Her skin was like moldy jelly. It shook totally and yet the wrinkles made it feel tense and almost scabby. Her breasts were thin and white and the nipples were flacid and hairy and to add insult to injury, quite frankly she stunk. Her lipstick was put on in such a way so as to cover her actual skin line and the entire scene was one of instant repulsion.

Before I could even think up a conceivable way to get out of the horrendous predicament Mary spread her legs as wide as she could and fanatically started fingering herself and panted to keep time with her finger. She grabbed my balls and penis and started screaming at the top of her lungs, "Fuck me, fuck me, fuck me you whore." I couldn't get hard easily but somehow I actually came on her pubic hairs which threw her into a further fit of rage.

"Impotent, impotent, impotent," she shouted. "You're all too impotent to put it hard to a beautiful woman like myself. When I was Miss Atlanta they'd come from miles around to take a stroll, arm in arm with me on the promenade."

Just then Sara switched on a little bed-lamp. I got to behold her questionable body in all of its splendor. It was a million times worse. There was a giant scar from her left knee up to the bottom part of her vagina and she told me it was the result of cutting out some infected tissue. It totally blew my mind.

Mary calmed down a little and asked me to eat her. I refused. She asked if she could suck me off and still hanging in there, I told her yes. She didn't do too badly but who cared at that point.

Then came the really heavy scene. She asked me if I wanted to be her lover for $100 per day salary plus expenses. She described in lucid detail her plans. She wanted to get a cabin on a Swedish ship that would travel throughout South America and the Caribbean and have me take her to dinner, to her shuffle-board lessons, to fuck her and to be seen with her. I could have other girlfriends as long as I didn't keep them publicly and as long as they didn't detract from her pleasure with me. In a sense my social life was subject to and conditional upon her emotional and physical needs. Whether this deal was on the level or not, I don't know but her further statements that she was a disinherited niece of a Coca Cola executive seemed to stand the test of time and it turned out that the woman was extremely "well-to-do".

She said the deal would last for sixty days and afterward, if I was still into her and she still into me I could stay on with her in Atlanta, she'd keep me alive and would care for me like a lover-mother. It sounded crazy and I considered the sixty-day part of the package but somehow my morality told me to get my fuckin' clothes on and get the fuck out while the running was good.

I told her no and she began to beg and plead with me to do something to make her feel loved and wanted. She told me that she had the needs and desires and hopes of any sexual being and she shouldn't be denied simply because of her wrinkling body. Shades of Marla Swenson. She was right but I advised her that she should have prepared for the wrinkles a long time ago, something that I myself was preparing for at that very moment. I figured to myself that if anyone could look like Sara did that night, I better start preparing for the long physical demise. She asked me to suck on her boobs and when I declined she begged me to just hold her tight and be kind to her which I did do. She fell asleep wailing and grunting and I did too, more or less. The next thing I knew, Howie, the roommate from hell was standing over Sara and me, and the look on his face was a strange conglomeration of shock, surprise, disgust and shame for me. He was also really pissed off that I came on his bed. Sara was all upset and hassled and threw her rag of a dress back on and in a quiet, concerned voice asked me if I'd decided to take her up on her offer. I told her that I was confused and tired and that I thought it'd be better to forget it indefinitely. With that I heard the loudest scream she'd emitted all night and then the most shocking words of all.

"I'm sixty-two you horny bastard. Now go straight the fuck to hell."

Howie and I, once rid of this maniac, went to sleep at once. We never discussed the situation again.

Richard V. Campagna

Chapter XXVI

Marlene Maçedo (alias Lene Cedilha Cedo), age 21 weight 120

The next chick I made it with in Brazil was Marlene Macedo (pronounced Mahr-lehn-knee) and the outcome of our encounter was even more perilous for me than was the one with Sara.

Marlene's a beautiful girl. She's about my height and she's what the Brazilians call a mulatinha (mulata). Her skin is velvety soft, her hair super straight and shiny and her lips about average thickness. Her nose is very pushed in much like a little puppy dog and it makes her look cute and beautiful at the same time.

Marlene is also a part-time prostitute. When she's off duty she can be sweet, kind, moral, sincere and suffers from normal confidence problems. When she's on, she's mean, ornery, tough, precise with her business expenses and potentially murderous. I wasn't sure in exactly what role I'd met Marlene, so I assumed we were getting things together as would a boyfriend and girlfriend. The assumption was good until ... Well let me tell you the whole story. This too, like most of my bullshit, has no traditional moral but makes for interesting existential reading and offers potential guidelines for future generations.

One of the guys from the hotel, Goldie, also from Brooklyn, asked me if I wanted to go downtown to the Combat Zone and go drinking in some of the bars down there. He said that while downtown Rio, just like Times Square or Pigalle in Paris or Picadilly in London wasn't the classiest spot in the city, it was the place with the most bizarre occurrences. He said the floor shows were out of sight there, the prostitutes were crawling out of the walls and were fairly good looking and the bus ride down there was only four cents. How could I refuse?

When we got off the 107 bus we were right in the heart of the zone. The smell of pork and chicken and exotic fruit juices and coconut candy filled the air and the streets were lined with dirty, oily, scraggly beggars and drunkards and dwarfs and amputees and any other type of misfortunate you could conceive of. But somehow these people seemed to get by, day after day and somehow they seemed to have an "ecological" medium set up. In the background the somewhat gayer life could be perceived. A line of American and European and Australian oriented bars lit up the streets, with American pop and rock filling the air. In between the songs I felt like doing a radio commercial for old times' sake, but was more intent upon some heavy humping. In the doorway of every bar was a barker or two, a hooker or two, a cheap client or two who didn't want to pay his bar bill and occasionally one could see a member of the military police in to collect his share of the graft money. Pictures of the nation's most beautiful girls were seen all over, and competitive photographers and caricaturists could be found hounding any couple that looked like they had more than 10 or 15 cruzeiros to their name.

Goldie and I worked our way through the masses and

a feeling of self-consciousness began to hit us since we were attired so much better than everyone else. We were attracted to one particular bar, the Bar Scandinavia, because of one particular mulata out in front and when we eventually pushed ourselves inside we'd realized that we made a favorable decision. Scandinavia was the only bar with a live band and its girls were extremely cute and sexy. When we sat down we were immediately attacked by five or six of the house's finest, who were to vie almost in a cut-throat manner for our affections and money. The competition was so intense for the Portuguese speaking Americans that one of the girls who wanted to be with Goldie and was rebuffed, first slugged the victorious other girl and then in turn whacked Goldie on the forehead with her "bolsa" (pocket-book).

I picked out my chick, Marlene, immediately and Goldie then followed suit. All of the losing candidates immediately headed elsewhere. We sat there for about another hour, putting away rum and cokes and dizzily listening to Brazilian and American pop-rock. Before long the foursome was ready for the rack. I sat there and contemplated Marlene's naked body and even though I knew I couldn't conceivably love her, I tried to pretend as if I did, something I knew would make our sex better.

Each couple went their separate way.

Marlene really showed me an out-of-sight time. We went to another bar called Mr. John's with more strobe lights, more American music, lots of dancing and a pair of nude lesbians making love on the floor for the evening's "grande finale." Lesbians are probably the most erotic dishes as far as males go, which probably explains why a hooker-bar of this type would feature them.

They made love to a Hugo Montenegro hit and as each

one appeared to be reaching orgasm, Marlene's sly fingers made sure that I did too. Then she said that she felt   terrible that I wasn't going to spend the night with her, knowing full well that I'd reassert the opposite.

We left Mr. John's and went to a super-sleezy hotel for 20 cruzeiros, with morning coffee included and fucked the shit out of each other. Marlene wasn't even that good but for me she took the place of Jeanette. For some reason she didn't want to suck but wanted me to eat her. I was in a good mood and so to oblige her I had a little snack. I never really worried much back then about STDs.

I came bombing into the Turístico at about 6:30 the next morning. Edite said she was really worried about me but in my cutest Portuguese accent I told her that since I was a man of the world, I could amply take care of myself and if she laid off I'd still buy her some perfume. I eventually made good on my promise.

I saw Marlene the next two nights without fucking and without paying her the same 45 cruzeiros for her services. We were like boyfriend and girlfriend. I was helping her to live freely. Jeanette revisited. We saw two movies, ate some great Brazilian feijoada, played some pinball and kissed and held hands on Ipanema. I even danced, something I don't do too well and while dancing; we'd each speak to each other in our own tongues. And we did a lot of drinking. So what happened to ruin all of this on the fourth night? I don't rightly know the causes and effects but I can accurately report on the results.

On the fourth night we went to the romantic Hotel Miramar, overlooking the breathtaking Copacabana strip and beach. We drank, had some cheese and peanuts (the Brazilian sex drug), and listened to Chico Buarque through the fabulous quadrasonic speakers. Everything was extremely pleasant.

We took one of our normal walks on the beaches, took off our sandals, wet our toes and I suggested we go back to the Turístico, since I thought we'd be able to sleep together in a room free from roaches and with an outstanding breakfast. I should have never said that.

When we got there and the balding Cipriano realized that Marlene was somewhat slutty in appearance, he put his foot down against her entering. She blew up at him and accused him of being a racist. When I saw that Cipriano wasn't budging an inch I admitted defeat and told Marlene that we better forget it for the night and that she should go home and spend the night with her parents. Believe it or not, that's what drove her off the deep end.

She blew up and her Portuguese was so intense that I couldn't pick up all the curses and ugly words she flung my way. She did intelligibly say that I treated her like a dog, a mutt, a mongrel and any other word to describe a canine and then she said that I was the one from the gutter, not she.

I said, in stern Portuguese: "O.K., I can see that you're upset Marlene, it's time for me to get moving."

That smugness really threw the hooker into a further rage. She totally clawed at my shirt and then began tugging at my hair. And if that weren't enough she snatched my wallet, kicked me in the knee sharply and started running. That 5'10" chick can fly. I was so enraged at that time that I did something I'd never done before. I tackled the girl, and in order to get my American Express card and wallet back and to protect my scraggly locks I gave her an elbow in the ribs and then a cut knee. She returned with a flurry of punches, kicks and scratches.

Next it was my turn to run and I tried to get back into the Turístico and lock out "the whore gone mad". No such luck. She got in after me and reached for a huge brass poker and held it to my throat. Then the babe wiggled me into a corner, got some sort of trophy from the mantlepiece and held it in my skull. I wasn't feeling particularly cool at that moment.

"Eu quero dineiro, e agora mesmo! 100 cruzeiros ou vou te matar!"

(Give me money and now or you're dead as a duck.)

The conversation ended there. I promised her that if she'd let me run upstairs and if she furthermore promised to leave immediately I'd give her what she wanted. I was shaking like a leaf. Truthfully I was never so nervous in my entire life. Elifas, who witnessed the whole thing told me to thrash the shit out of her. I just couldn't do it so I advised him to calm her down and in the meantime I somehow came up with the blackmail money. She then decided to change her tune.

To this batty bird, the fact that I gave her money proved to her that I really loved her. Then she kissed me wildly as if I were a puppy and begged me to forgive and forget and to take her to another hotel.

I'm usually a forgiving person but she scared me so damn much that I literally ejected her bodily. She screamed and cried madly but I had no compassion. Goldie balled her a few weeks later.

Richard V. Campagna

Chapter XXVII

Roommate Howie

A in't all that much more to say about this guy. You
already know his physical state. As to the rest of his
life, the guy's a bi-sexual. He's very intelligent and
extremely sensitive and perceptive. Actually we've gotten
to be fairly decent friends most recently.

One night however he did try to check me out and see
if in fact I had gay tendencies. I woke up and found old
Howie about to insert his right hand down my pajama
bottoms and since I had suspected this for a while I
wasn't too up tight.

"Howie, if I catch you doing any of that shit behind my
back. I'm gonna break your wrist, call the unliberated
Brazilian Military Police and get you thrown out of this
male chauvinist city. Just leave me alone with your unso-
licited touching and get the hell to sleep."

Never any more problems with regard to that. Howie
got into more girls than he did guys in Brazil. And yet, on
the friendship plane, I don't know what caused it, but he
also really had a sense of kinship with the guys, ostensibly
for the first time in his life. His mother had screwed him

up beyond belief, so this was really good for him, being alone and far away from her influence.

Howie and I doubled a lot during the course of our trip. He had a girlfriend from Simmons College in Boston, he being a student of drama at the University of Miami himself. Not much else to relate—Howie was a worthy coin in life's register.

Chapter XXVIII

Roseanne Block, height 5'6", weight 122

After those aforementioned horrible and I really mean horrible relationships I figured I'd try desperately to get into something normal. I gave Roseanne a call (she was staying at the Hotel Regina, a little classier than ours) and I suggested we split the city for a few days. São Paulo was my choice. She was really up for it so I packed my tiny bag, grabbed a cab and headed for her place. She was standing outside in front and we swept her right in and headed to the Rodoviaria, the bus depot.

No hassle with tickets and bus schedules. We grabbed a hot ham and cheese sandwich (mixto quente or hot mixture), some Guaraná, the official Brazilian soft drink and boarded the bus. When Roseanne first ordered a Coca Cola they all laughed at her since apparently in Rio, Coke is rarely imbibed by humans and is used only to clean one's carburetor.

The bus ride route was like a microcosm of Brazilian society. We saw hills, mountains, flat arid land, small villages, mountain resorts, shacks, mansions, farmers, thieves and everything as we made the 200 mile trek inland to São Paulo, the industrial capital of South America and what will become the largest city in the world with 20 million inhabitants by the year 2006.

We got in at dusk and the city might as well have been New York. The pollution and the traffic and the noise were omnipresent on steroids. But it was somewhat exciting cause it was 7,000 miles from our respective homes. Yet after a Bahian dinner and a short walk, the excitement faded and we wanted to hit the rack. I finally found us a hotel for $6.00 per person per night and it was reasonable enough so we took it. Of course we later learned that the shower trickled incessantly, it only emitted luke warm water, we had no view, the night lights didn't work and worst of all there was no lock on the door.

Roseanne and I had been caressing each other's genitals on the bus so I assumed she wanted to go to bed. She did and we disrobed immediately and started to have some fun. Who should come bombing in through the unlocked door, but the bell boy!

"Anything I can do for you two love-bugs just let me know," he informed us in very acceptable English.

We told him that we had no problems and that we just wanted to be alone.

He left, but two minutes later he came flying back through the door with some forms about a tour being planned for the next day. Again I told him I wasn't interested. He came in four times in all and the fourth time Roseanne asked him if he wanted to sit in and actually watch us have sexual relations. I think he actually wanted to say yes but was probably afraid of his boss finding out. Finally he left us in peace, but taking no chances, Roseanne had amply barricaded the door.

Finally we tried to fuck. I was tired and while I was very excited about balling Roseanne I was probably a bit nervous. I didn't get hard too well and Roseanne took it upon herself to show me what she'd learned in her 3 years as a classy Californian masseuse.

She started to blow me and her technique paralleled Jeanette's. But she was even more skillful in that she had better control of my orgasm time. She actually knew not to suck too well or too fast or I'd lose my load in her mouth and not in her vagina. The subsequent three screws were quite excellent. Quite comparable to relations with Sandra Engstrom from Fairchild except that this babe had a together head on her shoulders. Her skin was also very soft and her shoulders were firm and curved. I didn't really want to see much of the city but the next morning we figured we'd give it a try. Not bad, not bad at all!

We visited the law school, some bookstores, an art museum or two, the Wax Museum, saw a concert, had some great coffee and lunch and eventually hit the beach at Santos, the resort city about 30 miles from Sao Paulo.

We had lots of sex the next night and the day after, and then headed back to Rio content. We had a really pleasant bus trip, met a lot of Brazilians and some Chileans, and spending the 70 some odd hours with Roseanne didn't cause any disgust or boredom to either party. This experience eradicated the other previously described interpersonal disasters. It turned out that we missed nothing in Rio according to the other group members.

Chapter XXIX

The next two days after getting back to the Turístico I went to the beach at Flamengo. The beach is pegged as being one of the most complete in the entire world in that it's got beautiful white sand, extensive soccer, volleyball and basketball courts, a swimmable bay with adequate waves and lots of beautiful people. The coffee and lemonade vendors abound and each one in his soulful voice has a song or a poem prepared to induce you to buy his wares. The beach is long and it invites contemplation as well as activity. The water is delightful, especially in the dead of winter which it was when I was there and the shells that line themselves up after each incoming wave give the illusion of a truly tropical paradise. There is virtually no odor to speak of on the beach and even a nervous soul like myself can lie on the sand, with no one around him and shift his contemplation from the sun to the sand to the mountains to the distant city of Niteroi across the bay. As I lay there I was at peace with the universe and all of its inhabitants and the sand in which I was immersed served to cushion my body. A better way to explain the phenomenon is that my body was just another grain of sand, trickling through time and space. I felt as though I was temporarily suspended from action and there was no one

Richard V. Campagna

running the show.

Won't bore you too much with the people I met that day. There were three, Sonia María Rodrigues, Josilda dos Santos Peçanha, and Maarten van Delft from Utrecht, Holland. One was a student, one was another prostitute and old Marty, the Dutch Marty was, fascinatingly enough, a radio man on a research grant in Brazil. While the two girls wanted Marty and I to take them out and play with them in the sand, I had a better time talking to Marty, especially since his mastery of the English language was remarkable. What we did then was to take the girls' numbers and we furthermore made dates with them for that evening at the Bolero nightclub on the swanky Copacabana strip. Marty and I had a dynamic time on the beach that afternoon and we actually had the nerve to play some soccer with the Brazilians who wiped us off the court. To regain our athletic confidence however, we invaded the basketball courts, picked up a Mexican point guard who was on the sidelines and proceeded to demolish three Brazilian guys who were already on the court.

Marty and I became very good friends and did a shit load of things together while we were there. He was staying in the hotel Inglés, around the corner from the Turístico. The restaurateurs and the prostitutes and just about everybody came to know us as MARTY AND MARTY-THE DUTCH-AMERICAN DUO. It was really good having a male friend for once.

Chapter XXX

Iexpected a lot more from the Bolero. Apparently it had become a decadent night club after twenty years of world-wide fame. The night show was foolish, the prostitutes were not even professional looking and the drinks were understandably weak and expensive. One thing however stood out and that was the band. The quality of the music and dancing in that club was inimitable. One of the hookers that frequented the club came over to talk to Marty and me when our two dates were in the ladies' room. She was from Nigeria and had danced professionally in Paris for five years and boy could that chick move her ass. Probably were we not with Sonia and Jo, one of us would have followed up on her. The night was an early one and there were no sexual relations. I slept extremely poorly that night.

Chapter XXXI

6/30/73 Lilian Arnaut de Cavalcanti, Height 5'1", wt. 101

Today I met, observed, had lunch with, drank cachaça with, danced with and met the parents of Lilian.

Her mind is perfect, her thoughts are vibrant
Her hair is sagged with awesome power.
If she were evil, she'd be a tyrant
But she withdraws; a shyly flower.

She draws respect by being earthy,
Her naive class just makes her stronger
Of my longing love she is so worthy
Without her I can't be much longer.

She doesn't know how fine her face is,
Nor of the beauty of her slender body,
And to me all she's ever said is,
My thoughts are feeble, my mind is shoddy.

I know better through intuition,

I've got the fever I've got the chill

I'd love her forever with permission,

She's real, she's gorgeous, se chama Lil (her name is Lil).

I know librarians are supposed to be tense and unsexy and have their hair tied back and be really into an introspective life style, but stereotypes are set up to be broken; Lilian sure put holes through that one. Either that, or they just don't make librarians in Brooklyn like they do in Brazil.

On the morning of the 30th I decided to take a walk downtown and see the little publicized business district of Rio in action. Downtown Rio is really a far out little place; little compared to New York, but big compared to most things South American. There are myriad bookstores, newsstands, maracujá juice stands, Bahian women selling their carvings and coconut candy in baskets perched upon their heads and dozens of other quaint little antiquities infused with thousands of nervous, well-dressed international businessmen trying to hustle up some cruzeiros in between cafezinhos and cheating on their unsuspecting wives. The buildings in the downtown area are large, certainly not monstrous, and most are daringly modern, consistent with the prevailing philosophy of the Brazilian military conglomerate—THE PAST MUST BE ERADICATED AND BRAZIL MUST TRAVERSE THE THRESHOLD OF MODERNISM.

You can catch the pulse of the country anyplace you walk, but most particularly downtown. There were only two historical buildings left in the downtown area that I could find—the court house and the library. To retrogress to the Brazil that I knew so well through my textbooks, I decided to duck into the National Brazilian Library on Avenida Rio Branco, allegedly looking for a copy of the Brazilian Penal Code which I happened to know was recently revised. Actually I was kind of hot and I also knew that the library was air conditioned (ar refrigerado). The time was 9:30 more or less. Before I got out of there it was 3:30 in the afternoon but it was worth it since I walked out with luscious Lilian, the librarian, in my arms. This delightful librarian, the vivacious and ever succulent Lilian Arnaut de Cavalcanti was from a proud family of washed-out Portuguese noblemen. She was also very fussy about the placing of an I at the end of her name instead of an E, for Cavalcante is the name of a long line of wagon makers and innkeepers. Enough of that. How could I even bore you with such inanity?

As soon as I beheld Lilian's smile I knew I wanted to kiss her perfectly shaped lips. Never before had I really gotten into the contour and texture of lips. But hers fascinated me. I figured they were just things you kissed with and nothing more. But I'll tell you, lips to me right now are a dynamically important part of one's appearance. They are what draw you in. And coupled with a decent personality and a normal body they can be a very effective weapon in drawing the first kiss. That's where the initial contact is made and that's where the romance is born. If that first kiss is a loser, odds are that the whole affair will flop as well. And a good creative kisser just can't be beaten. The first time I kissed Lilian's lips was on the top step of the huge spiral staircase of this monstrous expanse of a library. This place was probably the equivalent of our huge edifice on Fifth Avenue and 42nd Street in New York.

Lilian was so appealing and so different from anything I'd ever seen before that I became extremely stiff. But the tension probably also came from the nervous energy that mud-like Brazilian coffee produces and also from the excitement of mere physical presence in this remarkable country.

Before I get into Lilian and myself, let me just tell you what went on in that crazy hotel Turístico that morning.

Everyone gets awakened by this obnoxious buzzer that goes off every hour on the half hour starting at 6:30 and ending at 10:00 A.M. Breakfast is served every hour starting at 7:00 and ending at 10:00. One good thing is that those breakfasts are free but what's horrible is that everyday it's the same damn thing. The Brazilians don't get into our Anglo-Saxon type breakfasts. Bagels and lox aren't the order of the day either. The cariocas are more into getting woken up by putting down three or four coffees and maybe some bread, a hard roll or some cakes. That morning I had one stale roll, two tabs of butter, some creamy white cheese from the Wisconsin of Brazil, Minas Gerais and some dark, rich and potent Brazilian café com leite. That was the maximum breakfast that Francisco, the breakfast man would allow. Because he was deaf and such a sad suck, I didn't even want to try to get another roll or anything else. I was just happy that I didn't have to behold his unappealing mug any longer.

I chatted with Marty who klopped on over in his wooden shoes for breakfast, and with some guy Bernard who also appeared to be gay, and with crazy Sara, the previously described 62 year old, known as "A Velha Sara" to the Brazilians. She sat politely and didn't grab anybody's balls.

The rest of the 52 Americans in the hotel were even lamer than when I first met them and I immediately concluded that I wasn't even going to get marginally involved in any of their private lives since I'd get only grief. Anyhow I hadn't the time nor the patience to correct their hurting accents and misconjugated verbs and as I bid them adieu, each one in turn butchered his "Até logo," the Portuguese version of "see you later."

If that weren't enough to make me uneasy by the time I got to meet Lilian, the subsequent bus ride downtown certainly put the icing on the cake. The bus stop was right outside the hotel and the bus driver almost clobbered my toes as he pulled up right next to me. He looked about 16 and drove as though he'd stolen his license. He ran lights, cut off cars, missed some scheduled stops, crushed an old lady's finger in the closing of the door and eventually did hit the back fender of a car in front of him. In Brazil, the seeming absence of tort law precluded this poor commuter from getting the city to pay for the repairs.

This moron even had a fight with his own "trocadero," the change man in the back of the bus and called him a fuckin' son of a bitch for giving away all the old silver cruzeiros. I guess our bus driver was a coin collector. (Fudido filho de puta) is fuckin'son of a bitch in Portuguese.

I got off somewhere downtown, pushing myself between the sweaty, swarthy Brazilians and found myself on Avenida Rio Branco. And that's when I ducked into the library.

So adorable little Lilian was manning (or I should say staffing) this huge, Brasilwood information desk in the lobby and her face was the most passive thing I'd seen in Brazil theretofore.

"Bom dia," I offered. (Good day)

"Tudo bom?" she asked. (Is everything O.K.?)

"Tudo bem" (Sure, just great)

I then asked her where I could find the Brazilian penal
Code and she ...

WHERE IS SHE?

He sits alone, smoothes his knotted hair,
And wonders why,
"Why can no other touch me this way?"

He walks along the lake and sees his diffuse reflection,
And wonders why.
"Why can nobody else see me like this?"

He listened to the crickets and to the sparrows,
and to the wailing voices of the farm women.
"Why does nobody else hear like I do?"

She will come someday.
She will warm his claylike hands; and he hers.
She will make sense of his unharnessed body;
and he of hers.

Only then can he say,
"I have something that can be shared."
"She loves like I do."

Richard V. Campagna

Chapter XXXII

This is Henry Schweitzer writing right now and I'll be winding up this novelette if you'll permit me to call it such. I hope you remember me. I'm Marty's oldest and dearest friend, although when you were introduced to me, Marty and I were hassling out some pathetically destructive disagreement, which has, as you will presently see, become mooted. This story is rather tragic since Marty Feinstein is now dead and has been so for over a year. He would have been 28 tomorrow and were he alive today he would be hearing his 14-month-old child say his first two words in the English language. Marty never finished his book, never got to fuck Lilian, or Jeanette for that matter and probably never discovered true peace on earth. He, like his sister before him, died instantly in a freak automobile accident in which he was not even contributorily negligent, and throughout eternity we'll never know how he resolved the dilemmas that tortured him and to be quite frank with you, that still torture me and most human beings, if they are being intellectually honest with themselves.

He came back to America at the end of his summer in Brazil, his wife Karen found this book in manuscript form among his possessions, and as I read the work it appeared that in the midst of his encounter with Lilian he decided to bag the whole literary operation. But his "living doll" of a wife asked me to finish it off somehow and pleaded with me to attempt to make sense of Marty's chaotic life. I promised I'd do my best and even though Marty and I never got our friendship back to where it once belonged, I consider myself Marty's closest buddy. I knew him during our trek through the existential anguish and that's what was important. By the way I've got brown stringy hair, pimples and stand about 6'1".

Marty left Brazil after the little tour had ended and as always had a string of chicks a mile long to add to his computerized list. They wrote him constantly, begging for his hand in marriage, sending sexy pictures of themselves in bathing suits, and promising eternal fidelity. But the old fart was still unhappy. Yet somehow, his beautiful widow finally was able to corral Marty's roller coaster mind, and bean-stalk penis for that matter, and our wandering anti-hero actually settled himself down.

Yes, Marty P. Feinstein had experienced enough freedom at the age of 24, and his first real romance was a beauty. Karen was 5 years his senior but that turned out to be a total asset in the relationship, as any good Freudian will assert.

The two didn't have sex for over three months after they first met, something Feinie hadn't experienced since Hudde Junior High School. I once doubled with the two and out of the corner of my eyes I could see Marty gazing into Karen's eyes like he'd never gazed at anything else. Karen was a dreamboat, looked great in everything she wore, in any environment and at any time of the day. Her body did something to Marty as though it were celestial. Marty used to open car doors for her, spill his coffee

amidst his nervousness and the guy even altered his grossness in order to be a Superman for his love. The two rarely
left each other's company; they read together, even played
the sport that Marty hated together—badminton. They
were an unbeatable pinball team, pinochle duo and they
were marvelous travel companions. Together they saw six
foreign countries, fifteen states and four islands excluding
Coney, Long, Staten and Rhode. In the twenty some odd
months of their union, Marty had more communicative
pleasure than he'd had in his first twenty five years. And
what good is it—he's not immortal.

At twenty-six then, he tied the legal knot going against
his Libertarian instincts. Our crazy friend Ronan per-
formed the ceremony, Ronan being a legal minister in a
mail order church; since then Ronan's been defrocked for
behavior unbecoming of a minister of God. The wedding
took place in Karen's parents' home in Goshen, New York
and it was really a "together" party. The Bauers live in a
stately old mansion on Fletcher Street in Goshen and the
pair are considered to be two of the most conservative hip-
pies in Orange County. They loved Marty, and the Marty
that the Bauers got to know, was not a fake Marty, but a
real, sincere and heroically tragic Marty. The same prick
that introduced himself in chapters I through XXXI here-
of actually painted the Bauer mansion twice, baby-sat
incessantly for Karen's younger mentally challenged
brother, Jay, and even learned to mow a lawn and prune
the bushes. Marty seemed to turn from an anguished
thinking machine into a relaxed, peaceful, almost blissful
feeling machine. His eyes changed from those of a manipulative wolf to those of a docile lamb. But this Marty was
happy. And the key to the marriage ceremony could be
said to have been that Marty actually popped the pus pimple under his nose. The pimple reformed itself, but Marty

whipped out the Clearisil and learned how to live with that nasty blemish without disregarding it, and at the same time attempting to obliterate it, knowing that such could not totally be accomplished.

In any event, the wedding reception was a veritable masterpiece. It rained for the first fifty minutes but the tent and awnings took care of that problem. And when the sun finally came out it shone for hours and reflected the beautiful union between bride and groom. Karen was dressed in yellow and her radiance seemed to reflect itself in everyone. Her shagged hair was incomparable. Even the haggard Marty radiated in his own crazy way. To be honest with you, Ronan and I even wept a little. 225 people showed their faces at the affair, and the contrast between the married couple was magnified by their guests. Countless dualities quickly sprung up: city guys, country babes, Jews and Wasps, polished duds vs. homespun clothing, and philosopher-academicians mingling with plumbers and jocks.

But the contrasts merely led to exercises in human oneness. And the party really swung, especially if the number of people who vomited in drunkenness is any yardstick. And subsequent to the marriage contract, Marty's life really began to turn around. One night he actually confided to me that over the years he had virtually lost this absurd nervous quest to try everything and that he was content with one occupation, one woman, one child and one Marty. If he really believed that, when his head went through the windshield of his friend's Mustang, then he truly came a long way in his brief trip on this carnal planet. Marty said "As long as I freely choose to limit myself, the limitation is actually liberating."

Marty finally realized the wastefulness of his quest and

yet the boss man up there still snatched his life out from under him.

I miss my friend. And I long for the day when we can be reunited somehow on whatever plane of consciousness. Whenever I feel weak I just remember that I'm alive and that Marty's dead. God, why don't you fuckin tell me what you do with all of these dead men and women. Do you eat them? Do you trick them and treat them like you do to us down here or do you show some compassion and merge them in with yourself? Why do you never answer these questions for us? Why do the answers only appear enigmatically on paper, in that goddamn manual that you call a Bible? Is that Bible any more true than this manual I've just concluded? Both can be destroyed in a matter of moments, just like Andrea was, just like Marty was, just like Roberto Clemente was and probably just like even you could be, if you'd come out like a man and admit that you're full of it. You and man are one and the same! You know it! Why don't you admit that you're as impotent as we are? Admit it, admit it, admit it!

What can we learn from the life of Martin P. Feinstein, lover, manipulator, linguist and liver for all seasons?

Marty has taught me that we can learn nothing of any lasting import from history, from technology, from politics, from love and from hate. Life is like a chemistry set with tons of chemicals and no labels. No matter what you mix, the same shit results. I miss Marty and I'll never forget his sister, Andrea, my first love. Who knows if I'll ever even come close to replacing either of them. I hate death and am ambivalent about life; it's like hating master and servant at the same time. But death is the ultimate master. No servant can run away from death. A Runaway Slave Law has no jurisdiction over death. We have nowhere to run. We are all Marty Feinsteins, we are all feeble sinners and thank whomever I'm supposed to thank that we have devised ways to forget our confusing reality. When I go I want to lie my weary body down next to Marty and Andrea Feinstein. They knew what it was all about!

Richard V. Campagna

Afterword

These are two pieces I found in Marty's possessions. Read them: They were part of his life and like all things in life they make up part of the existential mosaic of his affairs.

We have a letter-poem from an old girlfriend of Marty's and a story I assumed he wrote about a dinner party of love.

Henry Schweitzer

He sent me a prayer within a prayer

In a manufactured inspirational card lay his inspirational poem.

But does he expect my despair or my decree of absolution for his prolonged absence?

Perhaps he hasn't realized that I have cried the awareness of his self which I can't have. The heat and loneliness of the summer days marked this truth. From my desperation and dependence I grew to love his independence. He shocked me out of my stagnation which caused me to be sick for a while. But I am slowly recovering with a new, freer self to replace what I have lost and denied.

Yet the growing pains hurt and can be soothed by a

loving friend. In the process of freeing myself, how can I deny the freedom of another?

I only ask for kindness and strength; not eternity

Me

To Denise, my dinner partner, as we quest for the perfect dinner:

Once upon a time, in a kingdom often charged with granting contrived freedom to its subjects, there were two hungry people looking for a nice, hearty meal of love. One talked about how many times before she'd eaten some of that succulent love chow and how delicious it was. The other griped that he'd never really bitten into any of this exotic cuisine and with that, the two agreed to join each other in "feast of love."

The props were there and the table was lavishly set. Many of the couple's joint friends were there to experience the love encounter. But their presence became cumbersome and the aroma of the love stew was diverted in the presence of these onlookers. In spite of the encumbrances the meal began.

The girl talked endlessly about prior dishes of love she'd eaten and by the time she paused for her first breath, her dish of love was digested with negligible interaction with her taste buds. She bellowed onward about her prior dinner engagements and didn't even realize she'd devoured a delightful meal.

Meanwhile, the male of this duo was so nervous about not being able to digest this elite delicacy that he similarly wolfed down his chow, spacing out in the process, never even cognizant that he'd finally tasted the remarkable food.

Richard V. Campagna

A lovely meal went to waste and the two dizzily bid each other adieu as the midnite winds reclaimed their subjects and swept them once again on their separate ways.

The next morning both awoke, famished. They craved for the food that had eluded them the nite before. Yet each had to settle for a paltry breakfast in a local diner. But nevertheless it was rather odd that these breakfasts of mediocrity were so tasty and so real—so humanly digestible.

And the meal of love was wasted-lost to a ticker-tape of incomprehension. A meal of love, lost to eternity-a snack of mediocrity recorded and relatively lasting. It shouldn't be that way but the human adult is childlike and knows not always what's good for it.

The two will eat together again—perhaps next time it'll be so horrendous that they'll puke out their innards. But for love lost they alone shall pay the cost and when it's found the bells of joy will sound and the tip will be left on the table for humanity's hand to gleefully clutch.

About The Author

Richard V. Campagna was born and raised in Brooklyn, N.Y. He graduated from Brown University in 1972 with a BA in political science and minors in Spanish and Portuguese. In 1975 he concurrently obtained a J.D. degree from St. John's University School of Law and an M.A. in Ibero-American Social Thought from New York University. Campagna went on to obtain a Masters degree in Counseling Psychology from Columbia University Teachers College and a "controversial" Ph.D. from the American College of Metaphysical Theology after pursuing additional graduate study at C.C.N.Y., Columbia University, the University of Iowa and the University of Chicago (Returning Scholar Program).

Campagna is fluent in Spanish, Portuguese, French, Italian and Papiamentu and has a working knowledge of Russian, Polish and Catalan. He is an accomplished legal, literary and medical interpreter and translator. He also serves as a corporate spokesperson, legal consultant, psychological counselor and college and career advisor. He teaches law, economics and ethics at various institutions of higher education. He is an avid traveller, having visited all 50 states and dependencies (on numerous occasions) and 199 foreign countries.

Campagna was the Libertarian Party's candidate for Lt. Governor of Iowa in 2002 (running mate of Clyde Cleveland) and ran for Vice President of the United States in 2004, also as a Libertarian (running mate Michael Badnarik).

He has, in this book, edited, up-dated and re-titled his first novel, first written when he was 17 years of age, for the purpose of demonstrating how an optimistic, existentialist, libertarian and spiritual outlook on life is somehow essential and intrinsic to the human experience, throughout the life span. Perhaps, surmises Campagna: "as we get older, we all just simply get a little better at rolling with life's punches.............."

www.ingramcontent.com/pod-product-compliance
Lightning Source LLC
Chambersburg PA
CBHW030515260626
47157CB00005B/1749